Staten Island Stories

Johns Hopkins: Poetry and Fiction
Wyatt Prunty, *General Editor*

Staten Island

Stories

Claire Jimenez

Johns Hopkins University Press
Baltimore

This book has been brought to publication with the generous assistance of the John T. Irwin Poetry and Fiction Endowed Fund.

Printed in the United States of America on acid-free paper
9 8 7 6 5 4 3 2

Johns Hopkins University Press
2715 North Charles Street
Baltimore, Maryland 21218-4363
www.press.jhu.edu

Library of Congress Cataloging-in-Publication Data

Names: Jimenez, Claire, author.
Title: Staten Island stories / Claire Jimenez.
Description: Baltimore : Johns Hopkins University Press, 2019. | Series: Johns Hopkins : poetry and fiction
Identifiers: LCCN 2019011420 | ISBN 9781421434155 (paperback : alk. paper) | ISBN 1421434156 (paperback : alk. paper) | ISBN 9781421434162 (electronic) | ISBN 1421434164 (electronic)
Subjects: LCSH: Staten Island (New York, N.Y.)—Fiction. | Short stories, American—21st century.
Classification: LCC PS3610.I474 A6 2019 | DDC 813/.6—dc23
LC record available at https://lccn.loc.gov/2019011420

A catalog record for this book is available from the British Library.

For the Island

Contents

Staten Island Stories

The Tale of the Angry Adjunct

Today, on the way back home from teaching, I missed the ferry because the 1 train wanted to take its sweet-ass time at Rector Street. I stuck my head out the open doors, looked at the conductor, who was poking his head out the window. I told the guy, "Come on, man. What is this? Your union break?"

The whole platform, it smelled like shit. The conductor, he turned around, smiled, and blew a kiss at me. Then, afterwards—and on purpose, I'd add (I know it was on purpose because he looked over at me and winked)—he repeated into the loudspeaker three times, ever so slowly, "You must be in the first five cars to exit South Ferry, folks. I repeat, you must be in the first five cars."

All of the tourists came scrambling to the front of the train at once, like roaches, while the conductor's laughter crackled through the speakers: "Slow down. You with the Century 21 bags, don't hurt yourself now, miss."

"Jesus fucking Christ," I said. I sat back down on the train. I looked at the construction worker sitting across from me and reached one hopeful hand in the air toward South Ferry. "We're going to miss the boat."

"Always, with this train," he said, not even looking up from the *Advance*.

Then one woman, loosely wrapped in a 25 percent off Ann Taylor dress I recognized from the clearance rack, fell into the car because her stiletto got jammed in the gap between the platform and the door.

And when she fell, god forgive me, I just couldn't help myself.

I laughed at her.

Openly.

And with no mercy.

Because she had wasted three minutes, and the only thing I could do to prevent myself from screaming was laugh.

The construction worker, he helped her up from the ground and flirted a little, and the woman, she thanked him in a Staten Island accent, which had me like: Are you fucking kidding me? *Anybody* from the Island, ANYBODY knows you go to the first five cars if you want to get on the boat. What was she doing sitting in the back of the train?

Finally, 5:55 p.m. on the dot, the conductor decided to close the doors, and the train lurched toward South Ferry. Everybody—the students, the construction worker, the tourists, the little kids selling M&M's for "basketball"—crowded next to the door to sprint up those stairs once the train pulled up because we knew there was still a possibility.

We all stood there staring at the door clattering against the darkness as the train moved through the tunnel, thinking the exact same thing at that exact same moment: maybe we might just make the six o'clock boat.

As the train pulled up to the platform, I moved in front of the construction worker, and he snorted. The doors slid open. Then I ran up one, then two flights of stairs. By the time I reached the top, my fucking heart felt like it had doubled in size inside my chest. I pulled the door to the terminal open, sprinted past the pizzeria and the pretzel shop, waved hello to my dude at the newsstand who always hooks me up with the medium-sized coffee for the price of a small, and then swerved around a woman exiting the boat with a carriage and her two kids. I lunged up the left side of the escalator past the folks who had decided to stand, not run, up the steps.

The look on their faces was sad, resigned. You could tell they had given up on the six o'clock boat. There was no fight left in them.

But not me. I was going to fucking make it.

I started climbing up the escalator two steps at a time. At the top I saw the doors were open, and there was a fat old woman speed walking in front of me for dear life. The dockworkers, one white dude and a black one, pitied her, so they were delaying shutting the doors. Somehow the construction worker had gotten ahead, and I watched him enviously as he slid past the old woman, who had stopped to clutch her chest and breathe.

The dockworkers started to slowly move the doors shut. They were beckoning for the old lady, though, encouraging her. They were going to make sure she got on the boat, which meant that for me there was still hope.

I increased my speed, with my laptop in my purse and three folders full of students' work in my arms. My heart felt like rubber; the ache had stretched upwards into my throat. But I didn't care. I was going to make it. And then, because god all of a sudden wanted to be poetic and/or just, She, in all her Glory and Wisdom, arranged it so that I would fall flat right on my fucking face.

All of my students' reading responses, and I mean all of them, five classes' worth of paper, slipped out of the folder in my arms and exploded across the floor, disturbing a circle of pigeons deformed in various ways by city life: one missing two toes, the other bird an eye, this one's beak misshapen. A total disaster.

Lost: one expensive name-brand jumbo box of paper clips that I had stolen from the economics department during lunch. Missing: one free coffee coupon from Starbucks that I was planning on using the next day so as not to spend my MetroCard money. Gone: a tampon wrapped in the most translucent, greenest of plastics that had rolled next to the bare toe of one of those young long-haired dudes from the farmers market who was always wearing sandals, fronting like he grew the apple and handmade the cider when really dude was from Bay Ridge. I stood there, too embarrassed to pick the tampon up, then looked away as if it wasn't mine.

And the whole fucking time, the whole time, I swear to god, the two dock workers were laughing at me as they slid the glass door shut.

Now, let me ask you something: Does anybody heading home to Staten

Island have the decency—do they even care enough—to bend over to help me pick up my students' papers?

No. Absolutely not.

Why would anybody do something like that?

One woman even rolled her eyes at me as I picked up an essay that had slid next to her foot, like god forbid my loose-leaf touch your heel, lady.

In the terminal, I sat down next to a family of French tourists. They didn't know that they were destined for Staten Island, not the Statue of Liberty, and I was too tired to tell them otherwise, because that is always the way it is in life: you hope you are headed somewhere important and memorable, then end up landing on some strange, fucked-up island.

* * *

Stuck at the terminal, I spent the next half hour posting various articles about mass incarceration on Facebook. Only two people liked them. One was my little cousin and the other was an ex-boyfriend named Rick who still tags me in political memes of Joe Biden or next to the lyrics of old Mos Def songs. I was disappointed. I felt like this was a metaphor for my underemployment: here I was saying something big, yet instead of paying attention, everybody was getting married or buying a house. They were live filming their honeymoons, taking pictures of their children's bat mitzvahs at Snug Harbor, exchanging gluten-free recipes on each other's walls. But oh no, nobody cares about a thirty-two-year-old unwed adjunct or the think pieces that she posts on her walls, even if she is the author, or maybe especially because she *is* the author.

Later, after I got home, when my little sister Sam called me on the house phone, I asked her, "Did you see the thing with the dinosaur that I posted on Facebook?"

"Your cell phone is off," she said.

"I know. I still got to pay the bill. But who cares, you can reach me on the house phone... Did you see my post?"

"Yes, Lauren," she said. And then nothing.

"You didn't think it was funny, though?" I asked. It had been a meme of a pterodactyl which was supposed to be symbolic of the United States.

"Yes, it was funny," she said.

"Well, if it was so funny, why didn't you like it, then?"

"God, I really don't have time for this. I don't." She paused, and I pictured her small face, her blonde hair combed back into a tight ponytail. "Really."

"Do you not care about the criminal justice system? Or is the only thing you're interested in pictures of cats and your boyfriend Anthony?" Think about every stereotype about a girl living on Staten Island. That was my sister. It's probably terrible to say this, but if we were not related, I don't think we would be friends. I think that we would probably dislike each other very, very much.

"Listen, are you going to call Mom? Because she's been waiting for you to call her, and she won't stop calling me asking if you're OK."

I told her, "Look, she knows I'm OK. She just wants to make me feel guilty by having you call me to give the impression that she is worried that I am not OK. If she thought I was not OK, she would have called the cops already. You know that, Samantha. What she wants is for me to feel ashamed."

I picked up a sweater from underneath the table and smelled the armpits to see if I could wear it tomorrow.

"You *should* feel ashamed."

"Whatever. Can you please just like my Facebook status?"

"Can you be serious for a second? Just for one second."

"And every single status I post from now on," I said, upon which my sister hung up the fucking phone.

I stood up, shrugged my shoulders, put the phone back on the receiver, pet my cat, Chanticleer, and was like, *Whatever.*

In the kitchen, I peered into my dark little fridge. Perhaps there was something young and unexpired there that I could cut into pieces and place inside of a sandwich. I was thinking cheddar, but the orange block I found was bound tightly in some Saran wrap behind the unopened almond milk I bought last month, when I was trying to be vegan. And I was scared to even unravel the plastic, frightened of what sour smells the cheese would emit. On the other hand, this just might be a perfectly acceptable piece of cheese that was unjustly manhandled to the back of the fridge when I was unloading groceries. All of these things were possible.

My stomach yawned at that moment. I was so hungry that I was almost not hungry. The feeling had become unrecognizable and morphed into something else.

Fried eggs seemed to make the most sense, though this would require some work, specifically a clean frying pan. So I spent fifteen minutes scraping the residue of the previous night's pasta away from an old pot, then gently cracked each little unhatched chicken into the pan. The phone rang in the living room as egg oozed between my fingers and slithered onto the stove in the hole where the burner cackled with flame. In just two more rings, the phone call would be forwarded to the answering machine.

Alarmed, poor orange Chanticleer fell out of his cabinet. I looked at him and asked, "Can you pick the phone up for me?"

The answering machine clicked on as I was washing my hands, and there was my voice, girlish, small, silly, nothing like the way I imagined other people heard me: "Hey! This is Lauren O'Hare. Please kindly leave a message, and I will call back at my earliest convenience."

I was ready to hear Sam's voice, irritated, maybe driving to pick up one of the kids from drama practice at Sacred Heart, the sound of evening traffic on Victory Boulevard traveling through the phone.

Instead, the machine crackled like a radiator coming to life. Soap dripped from my hands onto the tile.

A man spoke in a low voice: "This message is for Lauren O'Hare." He repeated, "Lauren O'Hare. Lauren, are you there?"

His slow voice lilted just enough so that it seemed like he was on the edge of song. He paused between each sentence and seemed to intentionally rhyme my last name with the word *there.*

Normally, when bill collectors called it was one of those automated messages. A robot spoke asking me to contact them to pay some stupid credit card bill or student loan that had been killing me softly since I was twenty-one. But this guy sounded like fucking Dracula, and so close, I could hear him breathing, like he lived inside of the answering machine.

"We will call again," he said, and then the machine flashed red one last time and beeped.

First-person plural. How ominous.

And what kind of debt collector is this?

I looked at the phone number that flashed on the machine. It was unfamiliar, but when I researched the area code I noticed it was from somewhere in Nevada and remembered that I had taken out one of those payday loans last month to cover Chanticleer's emergency vet fee. But payday was only one week away. I'd give them the money back soon enough. "You'll get it when I get it," I said to the phone.

Then I smelled burnt egg and ran to the stove to scoop the scalded yolk away from the pan. Strips of egg white stubbornly clung to the supposedly stick-free ceramic frying pan I spent fifty dollars on last year, and it took a solid three minutes to scrape everything away. Fucking Macy's. What crooks. After a bit, I looked at my miserable dinner, the broken brown crust of egg white, the singed parts still stuck on the pan. Smoke had formed in the kitchen air—just a very thin trace of it, but it made things feel slow and evermore difficult.

My back hurt. The perimeters of my eyes felt raw from grading. In six hours I would have to wake up again to travel to the city to teach an 8:00 a.m. freshman composition class. The bus ride to the ferry would be fifteen minutes. The ferry ride would be half an hour. A man, the same man that always slept in the S62 ramp, would ask me for money. I'd give him one dollar. If I was lucky there would be time for a cup of coffee before boarding the boat.

Chanticleer jumped on the counter to inspect the stove.

"Get down." I dumped the miserable egg in the trash and went back to the block of ambiguously aged cheddar cheese.

It was fresh. Thankfully. So I ate three slices and went to bed.

* * *

Today my friend Jennifer, who adjuncts in Arizona, called and asked me if I had recently gotten a chance to look at my Rate My Professor. Immediately, I felt like I was about to have massive diarrhea.

"Just, like, don't freak out though, OK?" she said.

"Aw, man. Don't fucking tell me that, Jennifer. Don't tell me that!" I ran to my laptop and waited for its ancient insides to buzz back to life. "OK, just how bad is it? Tell me. How bad, Jen? Be honest."

"It's um—I mean—it's kind of bad. But like not really, really bad."

Which meant it was terrible.

"Why?! Why, man?" I was up for two different full-time instructor jobs.

"Just don't freak out, Lauren."

"I'm not, just—"

Finally, I pulled the page up and searched for my name on the website.

"Do you see it?" Jennifer asked. She sounded eager, which I took as highly fucking suspicious.

"Are you enjoying this? Is this, like, funny to you? Why were you looking me up on Rate My Professor anyway?"

"Oh, calm down," she said, but then she paused awkwardly in a way that seemed to betray some guilt. And then it clicked for me—we were applying for the same position at the same college because she wanted to move back home to Staten Island, and I realized that she must have been Googling me to size me up for competition. My own best friend.

"Jennifer, this is about the job, isn't it?" I asked her.

"You're so neurotic." But she didn't say anything else.

"I can't believe you."

"You're misunderstanding," she said.

Then finally the page opened, and I saw the review. My name: *Professor: Lauren O'Hare:* This particular reviewer's rating of me:

Poor. October 6, 2016: Um, I'm not exactly sure why anybody would rate this prof hot. She literally comes to teach in her pajamas. That's (a). (b) she's crazy (c) she makes zero sense and (d) she is just a terrible teacher. Terrible. If you want to hate English, go ahead, be my guest—sign up for Lauren O'Hare. PS don't get her talking about Medieval Literature or Irish ballads or else she'll break out into this corny accent and recite some old-ass poetry.

"MOTHERfucker." I tried to scan all of the kids in my current five classes I was teaching this semester. It was hard. I was literally teaching a hundred students. So, I tried to focus on the ones who seemed to dislike me the most, showed up late, or pulled out their cell phones during class.

"I think I know who this is," I said.

"Now, Lauren, don't jump to conclusions."

"No, I know who it is. For sure. I'm telling you."

"Lauren."

"Angela Deprimo. 6:00 p.m. EN 111. Freshman Comp. She hates me."

"You can't know for sure." That's Jennifer for you. Forever the devil's advocate, since fourth grade at PS 35.

"All right, whatever…Do you know what I wish? I wish there was a website where you could like publically rate your students in the same way that you can publically rate your professors on the internet. In it I would anonymously say things like: *Kid never read a word for class, but emailed me asking if she was going to get an A.*"

"Lauren."

"I would write good reviews, too, though. I'm not bitter. I would give props to the kids who deserved it. Like for example: For Omar, I'd write: *This kid works three fucking jobs, THREE JOBS, is learning English, and still shows up to class on time. What are you doing with your life, dear friend?*"

"Lauren."

"All right. I'm stopping."

"OK, just, you know…"

"I mean, why did you even show this to me? You know how I am." I looked back at the review, the glowing red F. "Aw, man."

"I just thought you should know."

"Yeah, you're a real Good Samaritan. Thanks... I'm not going to do anything about it. I'm going to be a good girl... I promise." There was a crash, the sound of a plastic bowl spinning on the floor. Poor Chanticleer had accidentally tipped it off the counter. "Look, I gotta go."

Then I hung up, pulled up the page again, and decided to write my own review of myself. It went something like this:

> *Obviously, this student is a big HATER and was unprepared for the intellectual rigor of Freshman Composition 111. I personally took Professor O'Hare's class and I found her to be a superb instructor. DUMB ASS. PS: Those weren't pajamas. They were very expensive marked-down Marc Jacob silk pants from Marshalls. Thanks!*

I finished my beer and pressed send. Then went to the fridge to find another one. But there were no more left. For a second I debated going to the deli and picking up a six pack—why hadn't I bought a six pack to begin with? God! The house phone rang again, and I scrambled to it, hoping it was Mark from the anthropology department, maybe asking to go out for a drink. But I didn't get there on time. The answering machine clicked and then it rattled with the familiar dark voice I'd heard the day before: "Is this Lauren O'Hare? Lauren O'Hare? Are you there? Are you there, Ms. O'Hare?"

Fucking Dr. Seuss, this guy.

* * *

In my night class today, we were going through the different parts of a sentence, and for a second, for a split second, I was standing there with the chalk at the board, and I fucking forgot the word *predicate*.

I mean, just like forgot it. The letters evaporated from my head.

I was like, "You know," and then I circled the last part of the sentence. "This part."

"What part?" Antonia said. She's this sixty-two-year-old Filipino woman who was going back to school and at that point spoke better English than me.

She was number one.

She was the best.

"Uh, the part where there is an action," I tried. "The part where things are done."

She looked at me, as if seeming to understand what was going on, that I was frazzled. That I was at a loss for words. And she said, "Oh, yes, yes, the predicate!"

"The predicate," I said. And then again, with a new sense of glory that the letters had surfaced, "The predicate!"

I rejoiced.

Then I thought that this is how dementia must be, the way a concept or a person or a word could at one point feel fuzzy and blurred and then the following sweetness once it has come back into focus.

Felix hit the ball, I wrote.

"Felix?" I said. "What part of the sentence is *Felix?*"

"Subject," Antonia offered. She was looking especially PTA mom today.

"And the ball?"

Complete quiet. Everybody always got confused about *the ball.* Nobody ever knew what part of the sentence *the ball* was. Nobody ever understood *the ball*'s role in the life of the sentence.

"Anyone?" I asked.

Crickets. Literally. There were crickets chirping outside in the darkening 7:30 p.m. sky.

"It is the direct object."

And then here was the difficult part of the lesson, the section of grammar that year after year always made my students tilt their heads and squint.

In a sentence, I explained, you can identify the direct object, because it is not doing anything—things are being done to it.

"For example," I said (and I always loved using this example: for some reason references to dating or love always made grammar click amongst eighteen-year-olds), "take the sentence 'Joan loves Edward.'

"Joan is the one doing things here. She loves Edward. She is the subject. Edward is the object because he is being loved. But that doesn't mean that Edward loves her back. He's just sitting there being loved. And we all know some useless guy who's sitting there just getting loved and doing nothing in return to earn it. And he, my friends, is the object. Sorry, Alfred," I said, because that day he was the only guy present in the room. But when I said his name and looked at him he jumped up a little bit and tried to put his cell phone back in his pocket. And I was like: "Alfred, really? Really?"

And he said, "My bad, Teach. I'm putting it away. I'm putting it away right now."

I couldn't blame the boy, though. Most of my students' attention wandered whenever I spoke about grammar.

Probably even your attention, dear reader, is wandering at this very moment.

* * *

Today, I was not feeling great because I'd just found out that one of my fellow adjuncts, Marilyn Rogers, had written a stupid fucking think piece about how Maya Angelou wrote shit poetry. It popped up on my Twitter feed, on the bus on my way to my 6:00 p.m. class at the other college I work at, and the thing was giving me heart palpitations. I honestly can't stand reading shit like that anymore. I x'ed out of the page and started to try to write a poem. But then something sucked me right back to her article and when I read further down the thread, I saw that she'd written, "It's doubtful that anyone can argue that Angelou's poetry amounts to much more than doggerel." That was it for me, man. I tweeted back: "Has anybody ever heard of a Marilyn Rogers poem? Huh? HUH? Where's your fucking poetry?"

Then she responded with a picture of an acceptance email from the *New Yorker*. My stomach knotted up into a ball and hate traveled through my chest to my shoulders and down my arms, leaving behind a chill as it moved away from my neck.

Liar, I started to type.

I just couldn't picture it. She was always typing these banal emotional posts on Facebook about her day or putting up pictures of herself giving money to the homeless. And then I was thinking, *Shit, what if it is true?* What if Marilyn Rogers did get a poem in the fucking *New Yorker*? So instead of that I wrote, "Even if this is true...whoop-de-do...you'll never be as famous as Maya Angelou."

Then all day I was worried that the head of the department was going to find out about my post and fire me. So I was preparing my defense / adjunct manifesto / exit letter.

Whatever.

"Intellectual freedom," I whispered to myself at the bus stop. "Inte-fucking-llectual freedom."

A teenager, possibly a student, looked up at me and raised one highly drawn-in eyebrow. Then it started to rain. And by rain, I mean that the sky pulled its skirt down and shit on half of Victory Boulevard. The wind toppled a garbage can and strips of paper, chicken bones, plastic bags, cigarette boxes, even a diaper floated down the hill and collected by the drain. Twenty-six minutes it should have taken me to get to the College of Staten Island. But instead it took an hour. The S62 had crashed into the limbs of a tree that had broken in half and landed in the middle of the street. The bus driver was this middle-aged woman with a tortured blonde bob who kept on saying, "Jesus Christ."

I went to the front of the bus and asked her, "How long do you think this will be?" Very respectfully, I'll add.

"I don't know. Whatta I look like, a fucking psychic?" She banged the steering wheel again.

"Nice. Really nice," I said. "Very polite."

She snapped her face toward me and said, "What?"

"I'm going to be late to teach my class," I told her.

"Well, excuse me, professor." Then she said something under her breath like, "Personal chauffeur," turning her Island accent British, suggesting that I was some type of snob.

"Nice. That's real nice. You know you make more money than I do, right?"

"Please."

"I'm living below the poverty line."

She snorted.

"I am. I promise you. What do you make? 50K? 60? You're going to have a nice little pension in a few years. Me, you know how much I pull? 22K a year. 22 if I'm lucky. No insurance."

"Lady, get the fuck off my bus."

She swished the doors open, and cold rain slanted on my legs.

Then a teenager from the back of the bus (probably a future student) shouted: "Ooh, shit! That bus driver told you."

His girlfriend had gotten out her phone and started to chant, "WorldStarHipHop."

I considered ending up a video on somebody's timeline for fighting a bus driver. While it was tempting, I had higher hopes for myself, specifically a full time job with a 401(k), so I said to the lady, "Fine, I'll probably get there faster walking."

And then I turned to the kid with his cell phone so he could record my comeback: "While you're still here, Mrs. Bus Driver, with that hair from 1992."

The kid's girlfriend groaned from the back, "That is sooooo corny."

* * *

About five minutes into my walk back to campus, after the driver had been able to maneuver around the tree, the bus drove by. The driver purposely sped closer to the sidewalk and splashed me with muddy water. I swear to god, on everything I love. I swear even on my cat Chanticleer.

I was late. Of course. Twenty minutes. Dirt smeared all over my coat and blouse. Some of my most loyal students were there: Karen Rodriguez, eighteen-year-old girl from the Bronx. Christopher Maldonado, thirty-year-old nursing student from Great Kills who looked like he was forty-six; Yasmin, who traveled on the S93 from Bay Ridge. Arthur, this black kid from Mariner's Harbor who would stay quiet most of the time, then shrug and put his hand up when no one would answer. My loyal ensemble. Angela Deprimo, of course, had left. Fifteen minutes. That was the rule. Students only had to wait fifteen minutes and then they could go.

They all looked up at me, smirking.

"I'm sorry," I said. "The bus." And then I pointed to the door.

Yasmin nodded sympathetically, even though she was coming out to Staten Island all the way from Brooklyn. So if she was on time, it didn't make much sense why I, who lived only half an hour away, would be late.

At this point there were only forty minutes left of class, so I decided I'd ask them to read their personal narrative essays aloud. This would give me a second to do a variety of things, such as (a) breathe, (b) wipe the sweat away from my neck, and (c) peel the wet syllabus out of my purse to remember exactly what we were supposed to do that day.

Yasmin went first. Usually, she was on my bus, and I'd overhear her talking about how she cussed someone out on a shift at Aeropostale. She had long black straight hair and bright pink nails and purple glasses. Whenever she got excited, she'd shrug, look up at the class, and give out a little breathy chuckle. Yasmin had grown up in Bay Ridge all her life. Had struggled with an eating disorder. Hated *stupid fucking boys*. Was resident translator for her family. Already had a fiancé named Boris.

She went up to the podium and started to laugh. "So." She looked up at us. "This essay—" she grinned—"is called 'I Need to Get the Fuck Out of My Apartment.' "

The seven of us still left in the classroom started to laugh as the rain swirled against the dark windows.

"All right, OK, hahaha. I'm going to start now: *Bay Ridge. Brooklyn. My borough. All my life. Algerian and proud of it. I live in a house full of boys. I am the oldest except one of the brothers who tells me what to do. My two little brothers, twins. I love them but I need to get the fuck out of my apartment, because nobody in that house cooks or cleans but me. And I'm tired of it.* That's it. That's all I got so far."

"Bravo!" I said.

Arthur and Antonia stood up to slow clap, while I whistled. Yasmin bowed and when she straightened herself up she smiled, revealing new pink rubber bands on her braces.

Then Arthur went and presented a narrative he wrote in the form of a series of haikus about killer robots, Mariners Harbor, Bad Brains, and his mother, who was dying of cancer, who he played video games with in the middle of the night. All of it, the whole thing, was fucking brilliant.

The S48
Took an hour to get me
Home from the ferry

Two dudes nodding off
On the bus awake to hear
A white ambulance

Eddie's starting shit
Again with one of the girls
Who hates him on the bus

I wake up most days
Wanting to go back to sleep
Crawl back in my dreams

I love my mom but
I don't want to be like her
Smiling when it hurts

Antonia had started to cry. And this time everybody stood up and clapped.

In the margins of my grade book I wrote: *Pitch a series of haikus about being an adjunct to* Cosmo*?* Do *Cosmo* readers care about the angry life of an adjunct? Surely there was some website out there that I could sell something like that to for fifty dollars so that I could turn my cell phone back on.

Overall, though, I left class satisfied and reinspired by life. I even caught the S62 in time. It was a wondrous thing. The light turned red, the bus braked at the crosswalk, and I reached the stop just in time before the light turned green again and the bus pulled up.

At night, the last S62 leaving CSI was usually loaded with students from everywhere: Brooklyn, the Bronx, Queens, the North Shore. And their families were from Sri Lanka, Ukraine, Nigeria, the Dominican Republic, Palestine, Mexico. There were kids from India, Albania, Haiti, and Jamaica. From Algeria, Egypt, and Morocco.

And all of us masses tired, huddled on the 9:00 p.m. bus darting home through the black rain.

* * *

I got back to the apartment at a reasonable time. When I opened the door, the cat hobbled toward me from his sleeping place in the broken file cabinet, shimmying his big old orange dusty butt across the wooden floor. Chanticleer was more dog than cat, a pug in a feline body. I scooped him up, plopped my purse on the floor, and nuzzled his stinky face. In return, he wheezed back gratefully.

We understood each other, me and that cat, more than anyone in the world. All I required was his soft companionship while I graded eighty-three papers twice a month, and all he required was kibble. I poured Chanticleer new food. Then he leapt from my arms to partake in the dish, noisily clattering against its metal sides.

And now, it was answering machine time. I turned on the living room light and pressed play. The first message was from my mother.

"Lauren, look, I know you're mad at me, sweetheart, but..."

I clicked delete and erased her from the machine. *Beep*.

The first ten seconds of the next message buzzed like static, and I was about to press delete, but then there he was, that same creepy voice from the other night again: "This message is for Lauren O'Hare. Lauren, Are you there? Are you there, Lauren?"

I stood still. My heart beat faster and my stomach turned.

The man leaving the message stopped. Another two seconds of static. Then it sounded as if he'd moved his mouth closer to the phone's receiver.

"I know you're there, Lauren." Pause. "Pick Up the Fucking Phone."

"Jesus Christ."

I stopped the message, ran to the kitchen, took a knife out of the drawer, locked all of the windows, and bolted the door. I thought about bringing the phone into the room, too, in case I needed to call 911. But now that little black box felt corrupted by Debt Dude's voice, as if he lived inside the actual answering machine.

That night I tried to sleep, but in my dreams, I heard him calling me. And in one of the worst nightmares, the phone kept ringing even after I ripped it out of the wall.

* * *

When I finally woke up, it was half past seven in the morning. My alarm had been set for 5:00 a.m., and I lay there in bed, very aware that I was supposed to teach a class in Union Square in approximately fifteen minutes. And yet, the trip from my apartment on the Island to NYU was an hour and a half.

But god: to sleep, to really sleep at that moment. How beautiful. I felt like my whole body was shimmering, as if water and light were rippling inside of me and to call in sick would be to disturb the wave of sleep I was floating on top of. The slightest movement might puncture it, and then I would have to sink into the real world. And so I didn't wake up to call the English department. And when I did wake up, it was dark outside. It was going to rain again, the fourth day this week. And though it was only 2:00 p.m., the cold sun made it felt as if it were six.

I considered my options for the day. I would need to call the English department and apologize, but this would require an elaborate excuse: some type of accident that could not be verified by newspaper, phone, or medical record. After a moment, I decided that the best course of action would be to tell them that I had had a minor seizure, nothing that they would need to worry about, but serious-sounding enough that it would be rude to doubt it aloud or question it by email.

I would be able to teach again on Thursday, I'd tell them. I'd explain it was just a small episode that was a symptom of a chronic, personal, and embarrassing disease that I would prefer not to talk about, especially since they were not supplying me with health insurance. That should do it! I signed the email *Sincerely yours, Lauren O'Hare,* went to the bathroom and pooped, fed Chanticleer, made a cup of coffee, and sat down to plot my second course of action: Debt Dude.

The first idea was to change the message on the machine. I recorded a new greeting. "This is Olivia Rodriguez," I said, making my voice higher. Then instead of working on my poems, I read an article that had popped up on Twitter from the *Times* about how in Russia out-of-control debt collectors would stalk the people who owed them money, invade their apartments, rearrange their furniture, torture their puppies, etc.

I looked at poor Chanticleer and imagined him defenseless, crouched in fear, alone in his broken cabinet while intruders pried open each one of my locks. Who would protect him while I taught my second, third, fourth class of the day?

No! This would have to stop!

Appropriate measures would need to be taken. I ordered two canisters of Mace on Amazon and reached for the phone to report Debt Dude to the cops. But as soon as I picked up the receiver to dial, I heard my mother's voice on the other end.

"Lauren?" she asked.

"Mom?"

"You picked up," she said, with the slightest pretense of tears.

"By accident. I mean, I was going to call the cops."

"The cops?!" she said.

And immediately, I regretted it.

"What's happening, Lauren?"

"I don't want to talk to you right now."

"Lauren, do not hang up the phone."

"I have to go. I'm busy."

"Lauren, I am your mother, and you will tell me what is wrong."

And then that was it. Just everything came out of me. "How could you vote for such a terrible human being? Do you *care* about anybody else but yourself?"

My mother cleared her throat. "I don't expect for you to understand what it takes to be fiscally responsible," she said hurriedly and angrily, meaning someone she was trying to impress was somewhere in the house. "You—"

"And you think this guy is going to help you? You honestly think that in real life, if this guy came through our neighborhood, he would sit and talk to you or Dad? You're a janitor, Mom. And Dad is a mailman. This man was born with a fucking silver spoon in his mouth. Never worked a day in his life."

"Lauren."

"And he's a racist. You voted for a racist, do you understand? You realize that, right?" I slammed the phone on the receiver just as the alarm clock on my laptop started to beep.

It was time, time to travel all the way to CSI to teach the night class.

* * *

Angela Deprimo was combing her long black hair with her purple tips, looking at the reflection of her face in her cell phone. She looked up when I walked in, then said, "You're on time!"

I pretended to laugh. "Ha. Yes, I am on time. Unlike your annotated bibliography."

She sucked her teeth. "Yeah, unlike your outfit."

Often, when I think about Angela Deprimo, I think about Michel Foucault's *Discipline and Punish*, and that terrible first chapter about sixteenth-century European torture. And I think of my own role as teacher/enforcer and how much I hated being punitive when I was twenty-four. But now I am thirty-two years old, and I am teaching a 4/4 at three different colleges, with 120 students, zero health insurance, and a PhD in medieval fucking literature.

Now, I understand the desire for punishment.

Just kidding.

Or.

Like.

Maybe not.

* * *

The Case of the Disappearing Spoons: A curious thing happened when I got home. I went to the kitchen to pour myself some cereal for dinner and when I reached into the drawer for a spoon there weren't any!

None. Not one.

Which I'm telling you was highly fucking weird. Because I could remember washing a whole bunch of spoons the night before. So, the question was: who used all of my utensils?

Chanticleer?

"Did you use the spoons while I was away?" I asked him.

He said nothing.

A thought then pounded in my chest and prickled in the palms of my hands. I imagined a man climbing through my kitchen window, dressed in black. I imagined him with a stocking over his head, sitting down and helping himself to a bowl of cereal through a little hole he cut out for his mouth. One bowl after another until he had used all my spoons. Perhaps he had stolen a couple and snuck them into a fanny pack strapped around his waist. Debt Dude.

And then, in a moment of dread, I noticed there was a light blinking on the answering machine in the living room. It pulsed in the dark like a heart.

God, what if he's still here? I thought.

I'd watched enough horror movies to know that this was the part where you grabbed the cat and climbed out of the kitchen window. But in real life, we are never as clever as the way we imagine we'll be in the movies. Because in real life there is no running away. You live in an apartment that you can't afford because every year the landlord raises its price. You pay rent. Barely. But you pay it, and eventually you will have to turn on the light in the living room, because there is nowhere else to fucking go.

So I did. And as the light swept across the room, I saw everything in its proper place. The blue couch with flowers. The TV on the gray desk that a friend had brought me from the dumpster near his complex. Chanticleer's toys strewn across the living room floor.

In the corner, the answering machine still blinked red, making me feel nauseous. But I walked over to it and pressed the button, because that's what big girls do.

The machine's voice buzzed to life. "You have one new message."

And then: "Hi, this message is for Lauren O'Hare." A woman's voice, but I braced myself. "This is Miranda McCain from the English department at John Jay. I'm calling because we enjoyed your phone interview last month, and, well, we wanted to invite you in for a second interview next week Tuesday morning, if you're available—"

I paused the machine and pressed rewind again and again. *This is Miranda McCain from the English department at John Jay.* I grabbed Chanticleer and rejoiced. Take that, Debt Dude. Take that, Angela Deprimo. Take that, Jennifer, my best frenemy in Arizona. I fell asleep peacefully for what felt like a very long time.

* * *

On the way back from my class in the city, I caught the five o'clock ferry, which put me right on time for my 6:30 night class at CSI. It was as if everything was going my way, finally. It was work hour number nine. But I'd be done at ten, and then I fantasized about going home and pulling out my interview clothes for the next day. Class would be easy tonight. Today, their final drafts of their personal narratives were due. Plan was to have them read their final essays aloud.

"All right, all right, all right," I said, walking into the room. "Take your essays out! Let's see 'em!"

The class groaned. Antonia had put hers in a blue folder with a golden embossed border, which she'd placed on her desk. Of course, Angela Deprimo did not bring hers in, and she made sure to make it very obvious to everyone that she did not, maybe would not ever, hand in the personal narrative. Then Christopher Maldonado was apologizing, saying he got stuck at work and that he hadn't had time to print it out. Could he email it when he got home, he asked.

I sat there looking at all of them, too happy to be annoyed.

I was like Oprah: "You can get an extension, and you can get an extension. You all get extensions! Yay!"

Later that night, though, when I got back to my apartment, there was a late rent notice taped on my door under the knocker. I looked down each dark hallway. They had not bothered to even fold it or put it in an envelope. So anybody who'd passed by would know that I was three weeks late. How many people had seen it? I ripped the letter off the door, leaving the Scotch tape with a piece of paper dangling from it.

Inside the apartment, Chanticleer was purring in the dark next to the coat stand, blending in with the umbrellas. I walked into the apartment and dropped my book bag on the couch. Then I turned every single light on in the house and went into my closet to find a pair of slacks to sew back the unraveling hems.

And then I heard it. The ring—and before I even picked the phone up I knew who it was. The caller's familiar out-of-state digits flashed on the machine, but I didn't care.

"Hello," I said.

"Is this Lauren? Is this Lauren O'Hare?"

"You know who it is," I said.

And then he laughed. "We've been trying to reach you."

"You have no manners," I said.

"You're going to be needing to get us that money right away."

"You'll get your money when I'm fucking ready. Now, stop fucking calling me. I have a job interview tomorrow." And then I hung up.

* * *

I fell into one of those sleeps where when you wake up, for a brief moment, you don't know who or where you are. But the light slowly started to remind me.

And then I jerked up from the bed in a panic to grab my phone and look at the time. "Shit!" I had forgotten to set the alarm.

The interview was at 9:30 on West 59th Street, which meant it would take me at least an hour and a half to get there by bus, boat, and train. I'd have to leave the apartment at 7:30 a.m. to catch the eight o'clock boat or I would be absolutely fucked, and it was already 7:08 a.m. I lunged out of bed, wet my whole face, and tried to wash it simultaneously while brushing my teeth. I smelled my armpits and could sense the dankness from the day before, but there would be no time to shower.

Makeup I could apply on the ferry. I threw that in my purse, slipped the too-tight slacks up my ass, and pulled on a long button-down. I grabbed a blazer, put my heels in my purse, and tied my sneakers on, because I already knew what would be required.

I would need to run. I would need to run very, very fast.

I was one foot out the door when I remembered that I had not given Chanticleer breakfast, and for half a second I agonized over it before running back into the apartment and spilling kibble into his bowl and all over the floor. Then I ran out of the apartment and slammed the door.

I sprinted for dear life down the building's stairs, almost busting my ass. From my doorstep I saw that my bus was currently pulling away from the stop. I ran after it, waving my arms in the air. The driver, a young Chinese dude with a thick Brooklyn accent who always drove the S62, stopped the bus abruptly, opened the doors, then looked at me and asked, "How come every time I see you you're running?"

"Oh, my god. Thank you. Thank you," I said. "I love you. You are the best."

"Now, don't butter me up. You better have fare."

I laughed and then pulled the MetroCard out.

"You think we're going to make that eight o'clock?" I asked.

It was 7:48 and we were about two miles away, but with traffic, who knew?

"Well, we could try," he said.

"Please." I sat down next to this old woman and looked at her. "I have to make this interview. I have to make it."

I cringed at the traffic ahead of us, and every red light made me want to cry.

"You will make it. Do not worry," she said in a Russian accent.

Then the businesswoman next to her, Puerto Rican or Dominican, short and middle aged, with her blown-out bangs and carefully painted eyebrows, added, "It's possible. I've seen this bus get to the boat in ten minutes."

Now, tears had literally started to form in my eyes. I looked at her. I said, "I really need this job."

A bulky dude with a DOT shirt turned to me. "You get there, just run. You can make it. If I get to the doors first, I'll try to hold them for you. OK?"

At Bay Street, the driver sped up and turned right before the light changed red. The people on the bus, noticing my tears, stood aside so that I could be the first one to exit the back door when he pulled into the terminal.

"Thank you," I said.

The bus driver let the doors swoosh open before he even fully stopped.

And I ran.

I sprinted down the outside ramp into the building. I dodged an orange cone that had been placed next to somebody's spilt soda. I am proud to say that I ran faster than even the DOT guy. But just as I entered the waiting area, I saw the doors beginning to slide shut. There was maybe four feet left of a gap before the doors would click into the wall.

And now, I had started to shout at the dockworkers: "Please, please, please, don't."

I started to say please so fast that it had turned into a hum of p's, like a prayer. The doors were only about two feet open. But I ran harder and slid through that small space.

The dockworkers started to laugh, as I panted and clutched my chest. "You made it, sweetheart."

Out of breath, I lifted a hand to say thank you and limped to the deck of the boat to cool down. Luckily, the wind had picked up, and I could feel the sweat evaporating from my skin. I'd reached into my purse to look for my CV and pulled out a whole folder of EN 111 personal narratives.

But just then, a strong gust of wind came and caught some of my students' essays, lifting them in the gray morning air. I reached frantically over the rail to catch them. But they escaped from my hands. Some spiraled downwards against the orange sides of the boat, while others landed in the cold green water and floated there thinly against the waves. The last of my students' stories the wind took far away, where they disappeared in the fog, to somewhere that I could not see.

What It Is

I guess you can say it all started in eighth grade. I got suspended for a week because I'd shown up to homeroom at IS 61 wearing a trench coat the day after Columbine, which, I mean, obviously—I know it now—was extremely fucking stupid. But in 1999, I was only thirteen years old.

To be fair, I was a little fucking weird, too. I was the type of kid who used to draw these cartoons of people coming back from the dead, until my English teacher discovered a picture in my notebook of a zombie eating his arm. Then two days and one phone call later from the principal to my asshole of a dad, and that was it for me: bye-bye, Christopher Maldonado. Mandatory counseling once a week with Laticia Watkins for the rest of the year. Then they put my ass in remedial, because at thirteen I still had trouble reading *Island of the Blue Dolphins*.

Now, looking back at it, that must have been the first strike.

A couple of months later, in November, I got caught huffing paint in the parking lot with Carlos and Troy by some Saturday school Regents Prep teachers, already angry at the world because on the sixth day god had made it so that they had to get up at five thirty in the morning to work. That was probably the second strike, although I'm sure there were plenty of other strange things that we did that year that made the teachers silently resent us. (What I've learned over the last couple of decades is that no one really knows the exact moment another person has begun to detest you. You can suspect it, right? You can think to yourself, That was *it*. *That* was the moment my wife really started to fucking hate me, when in reality it might have been years earlier, while you sat there holding her hand, watching Netflix on the couch, when secretly, unbeknownst to you, she'd been talking shit all week to her sister about what a scumbag you were.)

But I digress.

Back to 1999.

The day after Columbine.

In our defense, Carlos, Troy, and I had only been wearing trench coats because of a harmless and healthy obsession with industrial metal and *The Matrix*. Completely innocent. We sat there flicking paper footballs at each other, the volume on Troy's Walkman just loud enough that the three of us could hear the words buzz. I took turns watching the paper football game and admiring the way Lucy Diaz frowned as she tried to hatch her Tamagotchi, until suddenly she raised her eyebrows and opened her mouth in surprise. I turned around to see what she was looking at and the AP, the security guard, *and* the dean were just standing there in the doorway: "Christopher Maldonado, Carlos Lopez, and Troy Brown. Come." Then the dean flicked his wrist down to look at the time on his expensive, corny-ass watch.

One adult per kid, they escorted us through the long green hallways to the office, past the empty trophy cases where you could see the ghosts of pictures past—brief white squares three shades whiter than the rest of the background, where the faces of some honored students used to hang.

In the office the assistant principal had to translate for the dean and explain in Spanish to Carlos's grandmother that the trench coats were a sign of neo-Nazism. "¿Qué significa eso? ¿Neo Nazi?" Carlos's mother asked him, which in turn prompted Carlos to ask the AP, "What are you, fucking stupid?"

Poor Mrs. Lopez, she crossed herself. She thought that the dean was suggesting Carlos was worshipping Satan, which she had suspected to be true ever since the day he stuck his tongue out at the pastor when she made him line up at a church basement in Mariners Harbor to receive the Holy Spirit as punishment for piercing both his ears with a safety pin.

When Troy's father walked into the room, something seized inside of Troy's face. The office was well lit, and the transition lens of Troy's glasses darkened so that his eyes disappeared slowly from behind them. But even I could see from the way that the acne on his cheeks reddened against his white face that he had started to cry.

The conversation was brief. Troy's dad worked in construction and was stuck unemployed between contracts and didn't appreciate this shit, he'd said. You could see the dean getting nervous then and switching his tune up. So much for the expensive watch.

"Troy is an excellent student. It's just that, you understand, we have to be very strict about this..."

Troy's dad looked at the dean. "Fuck did you call me up here for, then? Unbelievable. Get up," he said to Troy.

And then I watched the both of them leave.

When it was my turn, my brother Danny had showed up because my dad couldn't escape the supermarket. So Danny had to drive all the way to West Brighton from the College of Staten Island in the middle of rush hour traffic.

Danny had played nice with the dean, and the AP had remembered him because he used to play basketball when he was at 61. But in the car, Danny was like, "Dad is going to *killllll* you when he gets home."

Which was true.

It was unavoidable.

There would be consequences.

"Anyway, what are you doing running around the Island, wearing a trench coat like a fucking loser?"

At home, I squinted into the TV as the newscasters showed footage from the Columbine cafeteria video where the two boys had come in with guns and started shooting. In the video, the boys were just gray dots, and everything was muted. They had subtracted the sound from the violence. I kept on squinting at the screen, trying to see the boys' faces, because for some reason I really wanted to know what they looked like.

* * *

When my dad got home, as predicted, he kicked my ass. Then he said, "And now, you listen carefully. I don't want you hanging out with that Spanish kid, you hear me? Stay the fuck out of Stapleton." Which wasn't actually the worst part. The worst part was that he decided to put me in Farrell, a school he had forced me to apply to in January but one I had felt pretty secure about not having to attend, reason being my father was broke. Now, if you're not from Staten Island—which the majority of you aren't and will never want to be—you probably have no idea what the fuck Farrell is, so I'll try my best here to capture the school in all of its splendor and glory. I mean, I could tell you it's an all-boys Catholic high school, and that might conjure some type of image for you which would help you understand the very basics of why and how it sucked. Maybe it's true that all Catholic boys' high schools are miserable, but I feel like mine was particularly wretched. Sit in a DMV for three weeks, have somebody hold your face underwater for a couple of minutes, stick your dick in a blender. All of these things were better than Farrell.

To put it into perspective, let me provide you with a roster of the ghosts of alumni past: Island Republican Vito Fossella, most notorious for getting arrested in 2008 after driving drunk through Virginia on his way to meet up with his side chick. Or district attorney Dan Donovan, who let Pantaleo walk in 2014 even though some Puerto Rican kid caught him on tape choking Eric Garner on Bay Street—a verdict, by the way, that my father, too, supported. "Of course they're not going to fucking indict Pantaleo. He resisted. Don't act like an animal, you won't get treated like an animal. It is what it is."

Half of the Island's politicians went to Farrell at one point. And though most of the kids who went there liked to consider themselves big shots, with their Thanksgiving Eve basketball games, the rest of the Island basically just made fun of them.

The cause of this disparity and lack of self-awareness? I do not know. Though I went to Farrell, I never considered myself exactly *of* Farrell. If pressed, I'd say I was more like a hostage.

What was worse was that my father really couldn't afford a school like that, so he harbored this bitter resentment that surfaced at awkward and inappropriate moments all summer long. Say I decided to sleep in on a Saturday morning. That afternoon, when I walked into the kitchen, he'd look at me and sneer, "Six thousand dollars."

Didn't twist the cap on the Coke tight enough? Wore the same shirt three days in a row? Dyed my hair red? Didn't matter what it was: "Six thousand dollars. And you're sitting there putting color in your hair like a little girl."

Almost twenty years later, especially after what happened to Danny, my father's still like this: inescapably angry. Say he takes an old friend out for dinner. They go to Joe and Pat's and the person orders the veal instead of the chicken parmesan, he'll fixate on those four extra dollars the whole weekend. It's ridiculous, and it's embarrassing, and I've told him so many a fucking time—I don't care.

Three weeks later, after he let me out of the house, I rode my bike down to the McDonald's between IS 61 and 27. I sat and smoked with Carlos and Troy, who both hadn't given up their trench coats, even though it was already the middle of May.

I'd seen them in school, but hadn't yet told them that my dad was making me go to Farrell. I already knew that Carlos and Troy were going to get to stay on the North Shore and go to Curtis, while I had a half-hour bus ride to the middle of the fucking Island.

When I told them, Carlos said, "You're going to have to wear those tight-ass khaki pants and a little red vest now." Then Carlos imitated the future me going to school and trying to adjust a wedgie.

"Whatever," I said. Then I got on my bike and tried to pop a wheelie, but my right foot hit the pedal accidentally and I lost my balance and fell. Gravel stuck to a patch of red ripped skin on my arm as I tried to pick it away.

"Poser." Troy spat on the sidewalk.

And I was going to say something back about him crying like a little bitch in the office three weeks ago, but from my place on the concrete, I had noticed that the bruise on his face had still not completely faded to brown.

* * *

Fast forward, first day at Farrell. In the cafeteria during breakfast, I coincidentally saw Alex Belinsky, this Russian kid, one year older than me, who I used to go to school with at PS 49 and whose ass I used to beat all the time at *Mario Kart*. It was weird, though. I was used to him being super Russian. Three years and all of a sudden he'd replaced his Russian accent with an Italian one. "Who do you got for English?" he asked. I looked up at the dude super surprised. His chubby fifth-grade face had stretched out.

"Adams."

"You're lucky. All you need is three P's to pass that class: a pencil, a pulse, and a penis." I pretended to laugh, because you could tell he'd been practicing that line all summer.

It turned out Mr. Adams was not from Staten Island, but from Massachusetts. Twenty-three years old, and it was his second year teaching. Really, he had never thought he would become a teacher. He had moved to New York City to be an actor, could not afford rent in Manhattan, then could not afford rent in Brooklyn or Queens, so now he rented the basement of somebody's town house on the South Shore. He'd told all of this to the class on the first day. Big mistake.

The boys OD'd on him in the locker room—imitated the upper middle class New England accent, an eccentricity on the Island where everybody spoke like somebody had punched them in their fucking face. Later they would give Adams nicknames: He was Asshole Adams. Faggot Adams. Adams Who Likes It in the Ass.

In class, when Adams enthusiastically put on these dramatic voices for Achilles or Agamemnon in *The Iliad*, the other boys could not hold in their laughter. Probably Adams had imagined himself to be the type of teacher in *Dead Poets Society*, a Robin Williams standing on a desk inspiring a group of boys disillusioned by their class and privilege. What this guy didn't get was that this wasn't fucking New England.

I wanted to tell Adams, "This is Staten Island, you fool."

Two weeks later, and I guess maybe this is the real point of this whole story, I met Pat Marino. He walked into Adams's classroom late, a junior track star who had to retake freshman English, then sat down behind me. Afterwards, Adams called on me to read this William Blake poem, and just like that I was back in a seventh-grade classroom, and I could feel the words waver before me on the page, slippery and unintelligible: *The Guardian Prince of Albion burns in his nightly tent.* My fucking chest felt like it was shrinking.

And then I heard him behind me, Pat Marino, whispering "Tent" in a girl-like voice.

"Sullen fires," I said as Pat's nasal voice trailed behind me like a shadow: "Fiyahs."

I stopped. I could hear some of the guys in the back laughing already.

Then I started over again: "Sullen fires across the Atlantic glow to America's shore: / Piercing the souls of warlike men, who rise in silent night, / Washington, Franklin, Paine & Warren, Gates, Hancock & Green; / Meet on the coast glowing with blood from Albion's fiery Prince."

That was only the beginning of the poem; there were like two more stanzas of antiquated English. The whole damn time, all of it, Pat was whispering behind me, and Adams ignored it because it was a fight he could not win.

* * *

After that, I tried to stay away from Pat Marino.

But unfortunately, we took the same bus. So I was blessed with overhearing such gems as: "I told her, 'You going to act like a nigga, you're going to get hit like a nigga.' "

I couldn't tell if he was talking about somebody black or a girl who acted like a dude.

Another time on the S53 bus, Pat had set his sights on a Puerto Rican kid on scholarship, another freshman, who he'd shoved as he walked through the aisle to the back: "Go back to Puerto Rico. You're on the wrong island, kid."

When I hung out with Carlos and Troy, I would tell them about it sometimes.

But mostly we talked about how fucking boring the Island was. And sometimes Carlos and Troy would slip into their own shit, you know, stuff that was happening at their school, that they were dealing with, and I found myself at the perimeter of even my own group of outliers.

At night, though, before Carlos would head back home to the projects and Troy's Irish ass went back to Rosebank and I left for West Brighton, we'd ride our bikes all the way down to the ferry from Forest Avenue, letting the downward sidewalk of Victory Boulevard take us there. No effort at all. We flew, no problem.

* * *

During this time, this is basically what happened at home. A speed version: my brother Danny quit college and started working for my dad at the supermarket. Danny had really been trying back then, before things had escalated with him and gotten bad. Before the money in the register went missing, before he basically fucked over my dad.

Danny was what they called a good kid, probably better than me in certain ways. Most definitely better from my father's point of view.

Danny could do things that Dad could not, like for example be charming, or like, you know, understand how to talk to people like human beings.

If Danny was working the deli, he was patient with the old folks trying to get a thinner cut. If somebody needed a price check, he didn't roll his eyes.

You want potato salad, not macaroni? All right. Not a problem.

And he'd charm the forty-year-old women with their kids in the carriages: "Anything else, sweetheart?"

There was this one man on a fixed income who was always short like twenty-five cents. Danny wouldn't even say anything to the guy. He'd ring it up, bag it, wish the old man good night, and put a dollar in the register. I know because one time I walked into Danny and my father arguing about it: "You do that, everybody's going to start to notice."

Danny lifted this meatball hero into his mouth and cleared a quarter of it in one bite. "Yeah, and then they'll come back because then they'll notice I didn't begrudge an old man sixty-two cents."

* * *

For a while things were good, but then Pat Marino came up with this new idea. It was like the Hunger Games before the Hunger Games existed. He probably learned that shit from the fifteen pages he read in *Lord of the Flies*. Rules were you locked the freshmen up in the locker room and then took two of them and made them fight. Upperclassmen made bets about who would win.

I heard about it first from Alex, whose wise advice was: "Just pummel the dude. When it happens, just take him down quickly."

"When does it happen?"

"Shush, man," Alex said, like, *The first rule of fight club is you do not talk about fight club.*

Alex Belinsky, still corny after all those years.

* * *

I had already decided if it came to it, I wasn't going to do shit. In my mind I pictured Pat Marino turning around to say something about it, and me trying to size him up in terms of what he would do if I said no.

Then one day it happened. I was changing last period after school. And I heard some of the older kids gather by the doors, a crew of juniors and seniors. There was only one other freshman next to me: Seth, a boy with glasses and brown hair, so fat and white they called him Marshmallow. Pat Marino stepped forward smiling and shoved him against me. "You hit each other, now, or we'll hit you."

I stood up.

I wasn't even afraid of Pat at that point, and I had not wanted to hit Seth, who was weak and cried easily during gym when Pat whispered "Fat fuck" lovingly into his ear, because I'd been taught by Danny that you did not hit people weaker than you. You just don't do it, because that ultimately meant you were a punk.

But Seth, frightened, came at me and swung, connecting his fist against my temple. It was the type of hit that just automatically makes you furious, automatically makes you want to kill whoever put hands on you. And so I landed on the boy while he swung his fists back and forth against my face.

Everything about Seth was soft underneath my hands. And the energy at that moment, between the seniors' cheers and the pain darkening the corner of my right eye, Seth clawing at my arms, the way he so easily stumbled backwards and then fell, wedged against the lockers and the bench, legs extended toward the ceiling, splayed like a cartoon—everything between these moments had built its own logic in my head, in which it seemed that the only correct thing to do would be to hit this boy, to hit this boy until he could no longer stand up.

* * *

I got suspended after that, and my dad fucking lost it. "Let me ask you a serious question, kid. What the fuck is wrong with you?" My brother Danny, when he saw the boy I beat up, looked at me like I was a piece of shit.

"You don't get it," I told Danny. "You don't know what happened."

"I mean, what else is there that I should know? Looks like you're the type of person who beats on people weaker than you so that you can feel big."

It was his way of comparing me to our father.

Later, I told Carlos and Troy about it, and they kind of didn't understand it also because guys like Pat wouldn't have lasted a second at Curtis. The North Shore would have broken a prep school boy like that in half. But they also knew I wasn't in the wrong here, not really, I think.

"I get it, man," Troy said. "It's like that's what it is. Sometimes you don't even get a choice about it."

Then one night, it was me, Carlos, and Troy with a whole bunch of their other friends from Curtis biking from Forest Avenue down along Castleton around St. Paul's, and we saw Pat standing there next to an empty parking lot, maybe waiting for a bus or somebody to pick him up. All alone. And I yelled to Carlos, I said, "That's the motherfucker from the locker room."

"Who?" Troy asked.

"That one. Kid with the corny Adidas pants."

There were maybe ten of us all together.

And Troy, he swooped down the street toward Pat to circle him. And then Carlos followed so that there were the two of them now riding in long arcs around him. The other guys flew right behind. Pat's face flickered behind their coats, which lifted and fell in the wind as they circled him.

"What the fuck, you freak?" Pat said, then tried to push Troy's bike over.

Troy swerved away from his fists, threw his bike on the ground, and entered the circle, while the other boys picked up their speed as they closed the gap that Troy had left. And now the ten bikes sped faster and faster and faster around in circles, my friends' coats now permanently suspended in the air, until the only thing I could detect of Pat were his screams.

* * *

I actually hadn't thought of any of this for a long time. I had lost touch with Carlos and Troy and hadn't talked to them in close to a decade. One night, though, I came back from my night class a little depressed. At thirty years old I had started taking classes at CSI again after things with me and Kathleen turned to shit. Then I'd started searching on Facebook for Kathy and noticed she was engaged and that Carlos, who had gone to school with her at Curtis, had liked the photo, so I clicked on his name and found out he was at med school at Rutgers. Didn't friend him, though. I wondered what, if anything, we'd have to say to each other. And Troy, his name, you couldn't even find it, because he had disappeared somewhere in the millennium.

But I did see Pat Marino again. He showed up at my brother's funeral and then the reception, lingering by the snack table like a fucking vulture. By this time, he had become a CEO at some Catholic Charities organization that was making the heroin epidemic their big thing. And opioids, the politicians were all over it.

Danny's case had made the *Advance* because he'd OD'd in one of the bathrooms on the boat on a Saturday and some little boy found him, his face sticking out from underneath one of the doors. After the boy had finished crying, he'd taken a picture of Danny's body and circulated it around the internet, so that the image of my dead brother's face had gone viral.

At the reception, after the funeral, I didn't recognize Pat at first. His face had softened, like all of his features had collapsed, like his skull had withdrawn away from the flesh.

"So sorry for your loss," he frowned, shaking his head, and then he looked at me hungrily. "Listen, Chris. You know we go way back, so I wanted to approach you with this first, especially after I saw that article in the *Advance*. Because you have a real point of view here."

It was so unbelievable, I couldn't help but laugh. It was like the guy had erased a whole four years of him being an asshole.

"And, god, that picture. It's a tragedy. But listen, buddy, we're building a task force to deal with the heroin epidemic on the Island. And I wanted to invite you to speak at a town hall meeting we're having. This is a time, right now, where we can really make a difference."

Then he went on about some lady who had just gotten busted for dealing fentanyl at IS 49. But, really, the bottom line (and we both knew it) was that white boys were dying of drugs on the South Shore, so the heroin epidemic was a popular cause.

I looked at him as if I couldn't place him right away, which made him nervous, I could tell. He was nodding his head at me even though I wasn't saying anything. Then I said, "Hey, remember that time you were on the North Shore after a track meet. Maybe two blocks away from St. Peter's?"

Pat looked at me, confused but hopeful. "I suppose," he said.

I laughed at that, the word "suppose" coming from his mouth.

I suppose.

Very fancy.

Then he looked at me even more confused and said, "I mean, I ran a lot in high school."

I nodded my head to encourage him, then said, "Oh, man, buddy, I think you'll remember this time, though. You were waiting for the bus in New Brighton. Just you. What were you doing out there all alone? Nice-looking boy like you from Princess Bay," I said. "And then you got jumped by these weird-ass motherfucking Marilyn Manson–looking kids in trench coats." I started to laugh. "That shit was hilarious."

He stopped eating his cracker. There were some crumbs on the side of his lip. Then he shook his head like he didn't believe it. But I could tell he remembered by the way he turned red. You can't forget a fist like Troy's.

"Yeah, you did," I said, laughing. "You know how I know?" I picked up a cracker from the tray and started to eat, too. "Because I was there."

* * *

That night I pulled up one old picture after another of Danny on my computer, searching his face for any signs or clues, as if I could will him to speak. As if I would be able to hear his voice again if I stared hard enough at a picture of his face. "Is this what it is? Is this it?"

I stayed like that for a while, squinting at the screen, flipping from his face, then to Kathy's, until their smiles overlapped with each other. When it got late, when I couldn't bear it anymore, I x'ed out of all the windows and shut off the computer, until the only face I saw reflected in its black screen was my own.

Great Kills

We only went as a sort of experiment and because my good friend Lisa Romero said she would take off from the tollbooth to accompany me. Besides, there was a promise of free drinks and food, and she'd never attended a high school reunion of her own. Fifteen years ago, Lisa ended up getting transferred to a Young Adult Borough Center in Brooklyn, so she was fascinated with the fact that I went to the type of high school with football games and proms. I fucking hated high school. I mean, anybody looking at me could probably tell I hated high school. It wasn't rocket science. I'd weighed no less than 185 pounds since I was sixteen.

But I was far enough from twelfth grade that a high school reunion seemed quaint and entertaining as opposed to painful, like an eighteenth-century tea party, and I thought it would be fun to show Lisa a little piece of my past so that she might know me better. We did that sometimes, went to places that used to make us sick so that we could laugh. Lisa showed up at my apartment dressed like a housewife with khaki slacks, a ribbed turtleneck, and a green and pink scarf tied around her neck. If you looked closely you could see the pointy top of a star she'd tattooed on her neck at the beginning of the millennium creeping up toward her messy hairline. Lisa was a good-looking girl, also super androgynous. With her broad shoulders, she was almost six feet tall.

"Welcome to Staten Island," I said. "So nice of you to dress for the occasion."

The shade of pink she chose to wear on her lips was horrifying, and it yellowed her teeth by contrast more than they really were.

"Some of it has escaped your mouth," I said, and I reached over to rub the color off her upper lip.

She stepped back and said, "I know. I did it on purpose."

I hadn't decided what I was going to dress up as yet. There was a part of me that wanted to look super professional and reliable, and I still had that in me. I still could clean up well. But then there was another part of me that wanted to walk in there pretend pregnant with a cigarette hanging out of my mouth. And another part that wanted to introduce Lisa as my wife. And another part that just wanted to show up and tip a candle toward the curtain and watch the whole thing catch fire.

I moved away from Lisa to pet the cat sitting in the corner.

"What's wrong? Your face just changed," Lisa said.

"I don't know. All of a sudden I feel dark."

She picked up a piece of junk mail from the kitchen table and spilled some weed onto the surface. "Don't sulk, OK? Whatever you do, just chill."

"I feel like ink," I told her. "Really, man. I just feel like pure ink."

Lisa raised her hand to stop me from saying anything further.

"Come, sit by me," she said, and unfolded her legs so that they drooped off the chair, then she crossed them like a proper soccer mom. I pouted and crawled over there, then shrugged.

Lisa patted my back. "Come," she said. "Smoke."

* * *

Once I was good and ready, I went upstairs and decided to get dressed up like myself.

When I came downstairs, Lisa said, "You look weird."

"How so?" I asked.

"I don't know, you look different, girl."

I went into the bathroom and stared at the mirror. My cheeks were full of color, and when I smiled, my eyes sort of exploded from my face like darts. The heat erased my wrinkles and made my skin look like it was ten years old.

"I look cute," I said, nodding my head.

She didn't disagree.

We ran down the hill to the bus stop. And when I arrived I had discovered that my MetroCard had run out. I started to explain to the driver that it was an innocent mistake, but she wouldn't answer me, so Lisa pulled me to the back. We were both feeling super self-conscious because a good fare-paying Mexican mom and her two-year-old daughter were sitting next to us. The smell of weed lifted away from my armpits when I dragged a hand through my bangs.

"You're twitching," Lisa said.

"That's because," I told her, "I am painfully aware."

The streets peeled away from the headlights in front of us into the dark.

My phone buzzed with a text from Jessica, who also attended the weekly NA meetings group at a little community center we went to in Bay Ridge. It said: *I'm in real trouble man. Is there a way that I could crash with you for a couple of nights? Please, Toni? Don't show Lisa.*

I showed the text to Lisa, and she laughed: "That bitch. She *just* tried to come and live with me, like I'm stupid and don't know she started using again."

* * *

Sometimes when Lisa came through to visit me on the Island, she'd jokingly point to a nicely manicured yard and a pool and say, "Look, how exotic."

If she was really feeling funny that day, sometimes she'd turn to me and say, "Jesus Christ—nice-looking white girl like you—what the fuck happened?"

Then she'd pretend to be Oprah: "I just want to understand what exactly happened to you in your childhood."

I'd shrug and lift both hands up. "I was beaten and denied food."

Then she would say, "It seems to me, Antoinette, that you are full of shit." She'd turn to the rest of the bus. "Anybody else here think that Toni is full of shit?"

People would dramatically look down at their newspapers or put their headphones on to pretend like they couldn't hear us.

"Oh, dear, Antoinette, it seems like everybody else in the audience is raising their hand."

I'd look around the bus and there would be like five people at any given moment who hated us, who probably wanted to see us dead.

"Tell me what was is it like, growing up in... wait, where the fuck did you grow up again?"

"Great Kills."

"Tell me about Great Kills," Lisa said.

"It's a dump. Literally."

One of the largest landfills in the United States. I remember our social studies teacher explaining how it used to be one of the few things you could see from space.

"Take me to it," Lisa said.

So, when my car was still in business, before it gave up on my ass, six thirty in the morning on the way to work, I drove her deep into the Island, all the way next to the mall. Even though they had closed the dump a long time ago, you could still smell it, all the trash that they had built a park over to cover up the stink.

"That's something that will never go away," Lisa said. "Anyways, who lets their kids play in that park? That shit is probably full of cancer."

On the way back we passed my mom's house, and I parked the car outside of it. It was dark and from outside I could see her picking up my son, walking back and forth with him in the kitchen, at one point lifting his three-year-old body in the air and then bringing his face down to kiss it.

After we left, Lisa said, "Ha. But a wealthy dump!"

"Well," I said. "More like middle class."

Lisa sucked her teeth and rolled her eyes at me. "That's rich, ho. Stop playing."

"OK," I said. I let her have it.

Lisa's own story was this. Her older brother had died in 9/11, when she was fifteeen years old. At the community center, the first time I heard her speak, she said: "My own mother says that god chose the wrong one—he should have chosen you, she says to me. That's why I get so depressed. But I guess my dad would say that's all an excuse. Every time you drink or you use, the devil wins. Still, I think about it, how my own mother says that to me. And it's true I've done some bad shit. When it was bad, when it was really bad, I stole from my mom. I even hit her once. But you know what, that was a long time ago. I'm paying for it and will pay for it. Everybody gotta answer to god, whatever god you worship, whoever he is to you. I don't care what *him* he *is*, eventually he's gonna make you explain."

* * *

We took the bus all the way to New Dorp and ended up wandering from one street to the next, occasionally running through the dark lawns of other people's houses to avoid their sprinklers. You could smell the grass and the worms stirring in the clean wet dirt. Fat fireflies bobbed in the dark, and once when I was running I felt their bodies bounce off my forehead. For a minute I saw myself as a car traveling at high speed and the fireflies bursting against my windows, and I thought maybe we should just call it a night and go home.

Some days that was how it was. I didn't even have the attention span to peel a piece of cheese away from its sleeve. I could sit on the couch and stare at the wall for almost an hour. Sometimes I would catch my mouth moving, remembering some argument I was having with my mom about money or going to see my son. Or not going to see my son.

For a while now I had not said anything to Lisa at all.

I turned to look at her and Lisa was standing there, full of so much hope, next to somebody's open pool, full of so much expectation for a party.

I dragged her away before she tried to jump in.

"When we get there, you should tell them that you're CIA," Lisa said. Lately, she'd been obsessed with the CIA. She'd been practicing making her fingers stronger by squeezing a bright orange grip strengthener at night when she worked the tollbooth in order to step up her jiu jitsu game.

"And I'm going to pick out the bitch who called me fat in ninth grade. I want you to fart next to her, then take her wallet."

"OK," Lisa said. "I will. I will definitely do that for you, girl. I got you. But then I want you to find your favorite teacher there and seduce him," she said.

"It was a woman. Mrs. Acker. She was a guidance counselor."

"I want you to seduce her then."

"No, I like her too much for that."

"All right, then, I want you to seduce your least favorite teacher."

But then I searched my purse for the address of the restaurant and I couldn't find the old receipt I'd written it down on.

"It's around here though. I know it for sure."

"It's *around* here?" Lisa's brown eyes popped wider. "What the fuck type of directions is that? I'm hungry, girl."

So we walked up and down New Dorp Lane trying to find the restaurant. But the street was different than what I had remembered it as growing up. It used to be just family-owned shops. Now, there were all these upscale restaurants. The Island over the last few years had been trying to upgrade itself, maybe trying to look more like Manhattan—which when you think about is such a fucking Staten Island thing to do. There was this one long and wide Chinese restaurant full of green and gold light inside. It was too beautiful to be where we were headed. So I didn't even bother to go inside.

Lisa stopped to bum a cigarette from this teenager leaning on a meter, then got pissed because the kid tried to charge her a dollar twenty-five for the loosey.

"I should just beat you up for that cigarette, you little shit," she said, adjusting the pink and green scarf around her neck.

"Go 'head, old woman," he clapped back.

Until I had to drag her away. That put Lisa in a little bit of a bad mood. Now, she was just looking for a fight. At one point we passed by this couple and this tall dude was getting handsy with the girlfriend. He'd grabbed the top of her arm and they were shouting. And Lisa said, "Hey, hey, hey. What are you doing to her?" Her Brooklyn accent surprising them.

The man turned around and said, "Mind your own fucking business, lady."

And that really set her off.

"Oh yeah, you like abusing women," Lisa said. "You like hurting women?" Which was definitely something we had heard in a movie once.

Then the girl looked at Lisa and said in a super Staten Island accent, the powder foundation on her face turning slightly blue from the deli's blinking lottery sign, "He's not abusing me."

Lisa's face grew completely still except for her left eye, which twitched a little bit.

"All right, fuck you too, then," she said. Then she waved a hand at her and turned around to walk away.

"What did you just say?" The dude lurched toward Lisa like he was going to do something about it, and I had to snatch her up real quick because she would have finished it. It was easy to underestimate Lisa, especially in her soccer mom outfit, without realizing she was fifteen types of crazy.

"That's what I get for trying to do the right thing," she said as we walked further down New Dorp Lane. "That's what I get for trying to be a sweetheart."

* * *

After that I walked into a couple of other bars expecting to recognize some girl from school and to point to her and say, "Look, Lisa, that's who I went to school with, see that girl, the frosted tips, that accent, her stupid jewelry, this is where I come from." But every time I walked into a restaurant, there was only the hostess cringing at both of us. We had started to give up, then spent a half hour trying to figure out what bus to take home, because by that time we couldn't remember how we'd gotten there.

* * *

But then I heard it.

"Oh, my fucking god. Is that Toni Figueroa? Oh my god, Toni!"

I turned around and it was little Leslie Cruz, who got stuck playing girls' football with me in eleventh-grade gym. Girls' football consisted of approximately six to seven girls who were all a little bit of a broken toy in their own special way. It was also highly unsupervised, so what usually happened was we sat on a grassy hill and smoked while the gym teacher devoted her attention to other outside activities. When she came around we pretended to run in circles after each other with the ball.

The last two decades had been good to Leslie. She didn't look much older than she did those days we spent pretending to play football. She'd rounded out a little bit, though, but had a little girl's face on a grown woman's body.

She hugged me and said, "God, you lost weight!"

It was a lie, but I thanked her. Leslie, the sweet little liar. She had always been a good friend.

"We're inside here." She killed the cigarette and pointed up. Of course, that was why we had missed it. The restaurant was upstairs on top of a bridal spot.

Lisa looked at her and said, "All right. Onward, little midget. After you," so I had to elbow her in the side. "OK, OK. You're right." Lisa put her hands up in surrender. "I don't know the bitch. I shouldn't be talking to her like that."

* * *

When we got upstairs I realized that it wasn't a restaurant. It was a cheap catering hall that was decorated like somebody's sad Sweet Sixteen circa 1999. The colors were pink and purple. Whoever had planned the reunion used actual streamers and balloons. Already, I saw Danny Delgado (fully bald, good for *his* ass), who'd mercilessly teased me for four straight years for being fat, dancing foolishly, with—oh, dear Lord—Karen Marino? One of the girls in our football contingent. But *why?* So pretty, long, wavy, red Julia Roberts hair, but poor girl always had such low self-esteem.

Leslie followed my gaze, looked up at me, then said, "I know, weird, right? The coat closet is back there." She pointed to a room next to the door we had entered from. "Hurry on back out. There's martinis!" She gave us jazz hands.

"Thanks, Les," I said.

And then we walked into the closet and got to work.

"Nothing from Leslie," I warned Lisa. "Don't even look at her purse."

"All right, I'll leave the midget alone," Lisa said. Then she pulled one wallet out and slipped out a twenty.

I was concentrating hard on finding Danny Delgado's wallet when all of a sudden we heard it: somebody shifting beside the room, then standing there in the doorway. "Fuck," Lisa whispered, but she had straightened herself out in .23 of a second. You would've thought she'd been praying in there instead of snatching up people's credit cards.

And that's when we saw him. Unremarkable, really, nobody who I had remembered from high school. But still there was something about him that was off right away. Lisa paused because she smelled it too. Because sometimes when you're a little bit off yourself you can notice it in other people, even when they try their very hardest to hide it.

There was something about his face that looked permanently fifteen. No wrinkles, just acne scars, one so deep and long it looked like somebody had slashed an inch off his chin.

When they write about things like this, when they interview the survivors, they always say that the people heard what was happening first before they saw it. The shots, or screaming, the confused bodies slamming into each other looking for a way out.

But we saw the gun right away.

We saw the man thinking about his gun.

We saw the man looking down the hall at the party.

You can say whatever you want about people like me and Lisa, but what a lot of folks don't realize is that when you've gone through the things that we've gone through, it makes you scrappy in ways that a lot of other people are not. Most folks go about their days and operate under the impression that bad things cannot happen to them.

But bad things happen to me and Lisa every day.

So, when the disturbed little motherfucker lifted the gun, I crashed all 235 pounds of my ass on top of him and he fell. I'm not a fighter, but there's a lot of me. And what I've learned is that when you take up space, that's a type of power, too. People think twice about jumping somebody like me.

And they fucking should.

As I fell on top of him the guy elbowed me in the gut, but now Lisa had wrapped her arm around his neck and was squeezing.

"You think you could just take people's lives away? You think you could just walk in here and take people's lives?" Lisa said. "You can't just take people's lives."

She had clenched his thin, pale neck between her upper and forearm, a move she must have learned in jiu jitsu.

Now the manchild's thin, long fingers were scrambling at her elbow. And she used her other hand to crush his fingers with her almighty grip. He screamed out in pain but somebody had put on an old 'NSync song and the party continued singing, unaware and painfully drunk: *It's tearin' up my heart*. During all of this, Lisa's scarf had come undone. It slid down the man's face, the edges darkened by his saliva.

"Woo*hooo*?" Leslie shouted out as she walked toward the coat closet.

"Where the hell are you guys?" When she saw the three of us sprawled out on the floor, Les screamed.

And her voice startled us enough that our grip on the guy loosened. The man gained momentum and stuck his hand out for the gun.

"Not today, asshole," I said.

But as I pulled the gun away from his reach, it went off, and the bullet shattered an old vase and lodged itself into the wall.

Hearing the shot now, the rest of the party came running to the coat closet reeking of margaritas and sweat and perfume.

Lisa grabbed his other hand and crushed that one, too.

"You can't just take people's lives," Lisa repeated. Her soccer mom makeup was melting unnaturally toward her chin, the mascara, the eyeliner escaping the corners of her lids, dripping down her face from the sweat, but also something else, I noticed, as I pulled his hands away from Lisa's face.

There were tears.

Eddie and the Dying Fish

All ninth grade, Eddie obsessed over the fish tank at the ferry terminal. After school, we would walk down to the boat from Curtis and Eddie'd pick out which fish looked like us. "I'm the clownfish, because I clown on you," he'd say. "You dwarf fish. You tomato, you."

It was all fun and games, my friends, until the fish at the ferry terminal started to die. Eddie was the first to notice the big purple one chilling upside down in the water. He pointed to the tank, and we squinted at its open mouth. "Shit, that thing is so ugly it looks like you," one of us said to Eddie. "Naw, that looks like your drunk-ass moms," he clapped back.

We all laughed at first. All of us.

We took turns making fun.

Sometimes after school, we posed for pictures in front of the tank, and one of the girls would throw the photos up on Instagram, where they would accumulate likes. But then the pictures of the dead fish got boring. We got used to it. Nobody laughed anymore. And at one point it just got depressing. All of those dead fish. Every week a new one. It didn't feel right.

Eddie said, "They're murdering the fucking fish, man!"

Then one day we came back to the tank and the old fish, the weak ones, were replaced by piranhas and other freshwater fish: royal green terrors, fat sleeper gobies, silver arowanas, river predators. Nobody noticed the replacements, not really. Not the finance guys or the DOT workers or the white bum that quacked at the tourists while eating bologna or the Indian dudes who sold pizza by the S74 ramp or the kids returning home from LaGuardia with their flutes and ballet slippers dangling from their necks or the prep school boys from Xavier at 3:30 p.m. making fun of each other's dicks or the rest of us hanging out by the Dairy Queen from Curtis.

Eddie did, though.

He looked at the fish as they squirmed in the tank. The stronger ones, the replacements, swam around like they owned that shit, which I guess, come to think about it, they did. And the fish, they pressed their one eye against the glass to look out at all of us, as if to say: "You, too, motherfucker, can be next."

The Knight's Tale

The minute Alex Delvecchio enters the store, Nicole starts showing off, roller skating backward with her blue spandex shorts and fishnet stockings. She has better clothes than all the other sales girls do, even the one with the wishbone septum ring or Lisha with her long black hair who comes into the store every day super Gothed out. We sell costumes, stupid glow-in-the-dark gadgets, and things like fake blood. Mostly, I work the Clearance section and the fitting room, though sometimes Chuck puts me in Key Chains and Mugs because I'm fat. Chuck, that's the manager, shows up every day high, wearing sunglasses, and smelling like an unmopped JCPenney bathroom floor. Halloween's coming up, so Chuck's always telling the girls to dress up, which actually means don't get dressed at all. The slob.

I don't have a cute costume, and I can't roller skate, but I've got superb teeth. And Nicole's mouth is still full of braces, so I believe I've got a shot.

Alex Delvecchio's one of those kids you always see outside the Applebee's smoking, throwing french fries at passing cars. He's got a tattoo of a snake on his neck and spiky blue hair. And once I sort of smiled at him, like this, nervous, as if I was hyperventilating or having an asthma attack, while I was waiting outside for my mother to pick me up. He didn't smile back so I looked away and stared into the parking lot at the landfill, at that big pile of Great Kills garbage wavering behind the heat.

I had a lot of things on my mind.

One of my friends, Katie, had just lost her virginity, and told me some things about it the other day during gym in a very cryptic way that made me want to murder her. Or snuff her in the chin. Not enough to hurt, but maybe enough to make her feel embarrassed.

She kept saying things like, "And then he…" She'd push her face closer to mine so nobody could hear. "You know, Arlene."

"What?" I whispered.

"*You* know," she said.

"I don't know," I said. "I don't *know*!"

Then Gloria D'Alessandro came in the locker room and started shedding her uniform on the floor like a freaking stripper. Katie looked at Gloria and then shook her head at me, showing off, as if the thing she didn't say was very obvious and didn't need saying.

So there I was staring at the landfill, in front of Alex Delvecchio, trying to think of something I knew that Katie didn't so that I could like *show* her I knew it and then not tell her about that thing either. I was thinking about how maybe I wouldn't invite her to the huge Halloween party they were going to have at my job. Or maybe I'd block her from reading my LiveJournal from now on. But could that possibly end our friendship?

And if it did, would I even care?

Then a car came by with a couple of posers in the front seats, and one of them stuck his tongue at me, screaming, "Here Piggy, Piggy. Here, girl."

Totally mortified. Like automatically, I looked across at Applebee's to see if Alex Delvecchio was still standing by the benches.

Thank freaking god, he'd already gone.

* * *

But here's Alex Delvecchio again! In the store, with Nicole roller skating toward him. And I am praying/hoping maybe he remembers me from that other day outside. But instead of doing something proactive, like for example saying hi, I just stand there by the key chain rack and the miniature glow-in-the-dark skulls thinking about all of the possible reasons he might be coming into the store. Like Fantasy #1: Alex Delvecchio saw me the other day staring at the landfill and thought I looked both beautiful and sad. And so he's coming. He's coming into the store because he just so needed to find out who I was. Like in that movie *Blood Buddies* where these two kids from Jersey fall in love, until the one guy realizes that his girlfriend's a vampire.

So he kills her.

Fantasy #2: The boy's shy. And so he comes into the store with hopes that I will help him find the appropriate band poster. But in reality that's just an excuse for him to get to know me. I smile, impress him with my extensive knowledge about all things music and unknown. Thus, he invites me to a show he's playing on Bay Street, slipping a free ticket into my hand.

Nicole gets to Alex faster than me. And I get self-conscious, because I'm wearing this old Kurt Cobain T-shirt from like 1996. (You know, the ones that say *RIP*.) And I only borrowed that junk from my brother in the first place because all of my ninth-grade T-shirts don't fit me anymore.

I am hoping, I am praying, that Alex Delvecchio thinks I'm just wearing this shirt to be ironic and not like that I seriously listen to Nirvana. Because actually, the type of music I listen to, almost nobody knows it.

That's how freaking cool it is.

"Can I help you?" Nicole asks him. She says it slowly and then smiles.

He shakes his head and then walks past her. And in my head, I'm like, Ha! Good for you, Nicole! That's what you get. Nobody likes your stupid fishnet stockings anyway.

Alex Delvecchio walks past the aisle of fairy princess costumes. The wall of fake severed hands. Past the werewolf and the zombies and the hockey masks. Past Keychains and Mugs, straight to the back next to the fitting rooms, where I'm the only one who can see him scanning the store.

And at first, the way he's walking around makes me think he's a shoplifter. We've had a lot of problems with that in the past. Once I saw this girl come into the store and try to walk out with two packages of vampire makeup. And not the cheap five-dollar kits, either. No, these were the deluxe edition kind with strawberry-flavored blood. The girl was too short for her wide-leg jeans, so she'd rolled the hems of her JNCOs up and stuck them with safety pins. The smiley face on her T-shirt had Xs for eyes.

When the alarm beeped on her way out of the store, Chuck tried blocking her from leaving. "Ma'am. You got something in your pocket?"

Chuck was at least ten years older than this chick, but in the store guide it says you've got to approach the shoplifter politely. You can't outright accuse the person of stealing or else they might sue for harassment, it says, which is why probably he called the girl "ma'am."

Lisha snickered. She was sitting at the register dressed like the Marilyn Manson version of Snow White that day, picking at a crusty Band-Aid on her wrist.

"Nope," Weird-Looking Shoplifting Girl said.

"Uh, I think you do, kid," said Chuck. He stuck out his hand.

Then the girl did a quick dance around him and sprinted out of the store and down the escalator. She was so fast that Chuck didn't catch up with her until the downstairs McDonald's. And when he did, the girl just pushed him on the floor, reached down, and stole his sunglasses.

Chuck scrambled to his feet, clutching his face as if his eyeballs were allergic to light.

"Security!" he'd shouted.

But the girl had already run straight out of the mall.

I don't even want to think about what might happen if I have to run after Alex Delvecchio. His legs are like very, very long, and I failed the fitness test at school twice because I couldn't run three laps around the baseball field in less than six minutes. At Our Lady of Mercy and Hope High School, there is no mercy or hope.

Alex Delvecchio takes one more look around the room before he spots me staring, then—bingo!—strolls over to Keychains and Mugs.

Close up, you can see his dark eyes are irritated and swollen. Raising both eyebrows at once, he flashes me a sarcastic smile before it melts away.

I try to look for my reflection in one of the mirrored key chains. Could there be something wrong with my face? What was it about me that made this boy want to smile sarcastically? I try, but all I can see in the reflective surface of the skull-shaped keychain is the hair in my left nostril.

"Hey," I say to Alex Delvecchio, smiling.

And then I stop smiling.

And then I smile again.

"Can I help you?"

"Do you know where the manager is?" he asks.

"Chuck?" I run through all of the different possibilities in my head: High? Passed out? Maybe sleeping in the back. "I'll find him for you!"

But in the stockroom there is no Chuck to be found.

"Probably smoking," I tell Alex Delvecchio when I get back to Keychains and Mugs.

He asks, "You guys hiring?"

"Maybe," I tell him, because I want him to think I've got some type of power here in this operation, even though I don't. "How 'bout I talk to Chuck for you?"

"No need," he says, then winks at me. Me!

And strolls out the store looking so freaking handsome in his orange fatigues.

* * *

For a straight two hours, I rearrange the wigs and masks in the back. I punch price tags on the superhero costumes, then count how many mummy outfits we have left. At four o'clock Chuck enters with two McDonald's bags and a giant soda, smelling like cigarettes and somebody's old towel.

"Some kid was looking for you," I tell him.

"Who?"

"This kid who was looking for a job."

"Was looking for me?"

"That's what I said."

Chuck puts down his McDonald's bags on the counter and sighs. "Always something with this place."

* * *

After work, I wait outside for my brother Lou to pick me up. Every now and then I look over at the Applebee's for Alex Delvecchio so that I can tell him I put in a good word for him with Chuck. Two seagulls fly across the parking lot fighting over a piece of trash, tearing it to pieces. And twice, I have to call Lou on the payphone and hang up before the fifth ring so I don't lose my fifty cents. But Lou, the jerk, never picks up.

It takes a half hour to walk home through the quarter-mile-wide parking lot, past the Wendy's and the Burger King and then along Richmond Avenue, which is just four lanes of cars. Two of them going south toward the rich part of the Island, then the other lanes going north toward the ferry. When I get home, Lou's stuff is all over the floor of the living room because, as per usual, he's in all ways useless. Like last month he got kicked out of SUNY Albany for selling weed.

"You're lucky they didn't throw your ass in jail. You're just very lucky," Mom had shouted.

"They're not going to throw me in jail for selling weed, Ma," he said.

"Yes, they could. They very well could." And then: "I spend all this money for you to go to this fancy college, and you end up selling drugs. What a fucking idiot."

When I finally get home, there's a sink full of dishes in the kitchen that he was supposed to clean last night. And I can hear Mom dragging the laundry down the steps to the basement. Ninety-nine percent chance Lou's upstairs sleeping. Ninety-nine percent chance he never really woke up. He probably let Mom do all the laundry, clean the bathroom, and vacuum, which is totally Anti-Woman of him.

So I march upstairs to his room. 5:00 p.m. and still in bed. The little blobs of his lava lamp slurping in the dark.

"It's your turn. It was your turn to clean." I throw a dirty towel at the bed. "We are not your female slaves."

He groans, still sleeping, then sits up and rubs his eyes.

"Come on, Lou! You forgot to pick me up at the mall."

"Get out of here with that shit, Arlene. Out," he says, as if that's going to scare me.

I tell him, "I'm not afraid of you." I go up to him real close. "You don't scare me," I say. Because he thinks he can do whatever he wants, which is what you call a narcissist.

"What!"

"I said, I'm not afraid." Because I'm not.

He stands up from the bed, turns me around, and then slips his arms underneath my armpits, locking my elbows into what they call a chicken wing. But I kick him, and when I do we fall backwards and smash his stupid lamp.

Mom comes running up the stairs saying, "Louis, let go. Let go, *Louis*." Until he stops.

Then he tries to pretend like we were just playing. "Just having fun," he says. "No big deal."

Ma drags her hand slowly down my face. "She's crying. You see." And then points at one of my eyes, poking it.

"I'm not crying," I say.

Because nobody makes me cry.

Lou throws things around like a big shot: his sneakers, a bottle of protein pills. He even lifts up his pillow as if he's going to throw it at Ma. (Which isn't beyond him, you know. Throwing something at Mom.) But underneath the pillow is a bag of weed, so he drops that shit quickly, checks Ma's face to see if she noticed, and then points at me as a diversion. "She started it," he says.

"Okay, so you beat up little girls now?" Ma says. "You beat up little girls?"

"She's not exactly little." He puffs out his face and extends his arms in front of him as if he were resting them on an invisible belly, mimicking me, that is. The jerk.

"I don't care what you think about my body," I say. "I have a healthy self-esteem."

"Okay, whatever, fatty," he says.

"Watch it." Mom raises her hand as if she's going to hit him in the face.

Then his gerbils get excited from her screaming and scatter their bits of hay. One of them hops on its wheel and starts to run and run and run. They all begin squeaking as if they are in a chorus. And I'm standing by the door.

"Mom," I shout. And when she doesn't hear me, I say it louder. "Mom!"

She turns around with her hand raised as if she's about to hit me, too. "What, Arlene?"

"I'm not crying."

* * *

Me and Katie are sitting in the front yard of Our Lady of Hope and Mercy sharing a cream cheese and raspberry bagel and Snapple peach iced tea. I'm waiting to get paid next week, and then I'll owe Katie three bagels, two hot chocolates, and five soft drinks. I keep track of it with tally marks on my binder. Basically, whatever I get from the store is like milk money for little things, like if I want to go out to eat with my friends, Mom says.

But what I really want is this sixty-dollar earth goddess costume in the back of the store. And if I save correctly, I can buy it in two weeks.

Katie pulls out a piece of gum and chews it. We're sitting on the bench by the flagpole, looking at *Seventeen* and waiting for the first period bell. I have the magazine out on my lap, ready to tally up our answers to the quiz: *Which Disney Princess Are You?* Although I already know that Katie's more of the Sleeping Beauty type. Me, I'm like Mulan.

But then Katie's got to get all boring and say, "I just don't know what to do," referring to Robby the boyfriend, that is, and how he wants her to quit the track team once she starts the tenth grade. She pulls down the hem of her uniform.

"You ought to be an individual," I tell her, annoyed, because literally just last month we'd read an article in *Seventeen* called "How to Be a Woman and Strong."

"Don't lose yourself for a man, okay?"

Then she has to turn around and say, "What do you know about it anyway, Arlene?"

"I know more than to let some stupid boy make me quit the track team."

"Yeah, 'cause you run track," she says.

Then we just sit on the bench.

"You're not even seeing anyone," she tells me.

"I am," I tell her.

"Who?"

"No one you'd ever know," I say.

Then I eat the rest of the bagel, which is sweet and creamy and salty all at the same time.

* * *

At the store, Lisha is pouting by the register, looking for Chuck to see if she can get off next week, and Nicole is looking for Chuck to see if she can take Lisha's hours. And I'm sitting by the fitting room waiting for Alex Delvecchio, who I'm hoping will come into the store again so that I can impress him with this new pair of jeans and perhaps make him my boyfriend.

It doesn't take long. 5:00 p.m. I spot his blue hair. He's waiting by the pretzel stand, and when Chuck finally shows up for work, Alex Delvecchio follows him into the store. My heart, it starts thrumming.

Automatically, Nicole and Lisha go at Chuck when they see him with: "Can I have such and such day off?" And: "I need extra hours."

He puts one hand up and tells them, "Not now." Then goes straight to the back of the store.

Meanwhile, Alex Delvecchio has floated next to the register and seems to be waiting for Chuck, so I wave my hand at him a little and say, "Hi," which he like totally does not even recognize.

Chuck comes out now with a stack of job applications. "Here," he tells Alex Delvecchio. "You happy, now?"

"Yeah, I'm happy." Then he slowly fills out the application and slides it over the counter to Chuck.

"You'll start tomorrow. But make sure you're on time. I mean it, Alex. I really mean it."

"I'll be on time like you're on time," Alex Delvecchio says, then walks out slowly.

Nicole doesn't even wait for the kid to leave the store. "So we've got a new guy working with us?" she asks, chewing her gum suggestively. "You know him?"

"Of course I know him," Chuck says. He grimaces at the application, then opens the register to count the cash. "That's my cousin looking for a job."

I let out a little yelp of joy. Then Lisha looks up at me like I'm stupid, so I cover up my enthusiasm by coughing.

* * *

My brother's dad, my mom would say, was a real asshole, not like mine.

"Your dad was a sweetheart," she said.

"Oh yeah?" my brother'd say from the living room or the kitchen or the basement, within whatever earshot of our conversation. "So why isn't he here, then?"

It was a legitimate question. I had often wondered the same thing, too. And I don't think Lou was trying to be cruel about it. I think he was genuinely curious.

Lou wasn't always a bad kid.

Fifth grade, I remember forgetting I had a science project due the next day. Mom had work in the morning and was too tired to deal with any of it. "You should have paid attention. And told me before," she said.

I was afraid of the fifth-grade teacher. She was a mean old nun named Sister Dolores, and I hated the idea of showing up in class without a science project. Lou knew this because he'd had his own bad experience with Sister D, too. Once, in second grade, she'd banned him a whole month from kickball.

Lou stood up with me, and we built a bridge made of marshmallows and toothpicks and straws. Around midnight, I started yawning, and he told me to go to sleep.

When I woke up I found that overnight he'd built the cables, the arch, the road.

It's hard to think of the old Lou being the same person as the new Lou. What about the world can turn somebody so quickly into an asshole? Or maybe he'd always been a little bit mean. When Lou was sixteen, he got suspended for smashing a kid's head against the window on the bus and calling him a faggot. When he got kicked out of SUNY Albany, my mom called my Uncle Richie to see if maybe he'd hire Lou. My uncle said, "Listen, Ell, I know he's your son and you love him and you can't help but to love him. But the kid's rotten. He's only going to give you trouble. Tell him to join the army or to get out."

* * *

"So you'll come with me?" I ask Katie. We're sitting outside again in the courtyard, Period Zero. Same place as always. Same time. Only now I have bought the bagel and the coffee and the juice.

"If I'm not doing anything with Robby," she says.

"Jesus freaking Christ. It's only three hours at most. It's a Halloween party. It'll be fun."

"Fine," she says.

Later, at work, I bring the earth goddess costume up to the register, and Lisha looks at the package with disgust. "What's this for?"

"The Halloween party at Chuck's," I say.

"You're actually going to that dumb shit?"

"Don't forget, I have a 25 percent off discount."

Alex Delvecchio is sweeping, pushing the broom closer to the register. I don't want him to hear Lisha making fun of me, so I pay for the costume quickly.

"Hey, Esposito," he says to me because that's my last name. "You going to that party?"

"Yeah." I lift up the shopping bag. "Just got my costume."

"What are you going to be?" he asks.

"An earth goddess!" I smile even though I can hear Lisha snickering behind me.

Alex Delvecchio squints at her, and I can't tell if it's because he's on my side or hers. "I just might have to be there then," he says, then looks at me and winks.

* * *

It takes me two hours to convince my mother not to have Lou drive me. "And I don't want to be picked up either. It's only fifteen minutes away."

"Fine, Arlene. Go," Ma says, and then she lights a cigarette and opens a can of tomatoes.

Later, when I walk down the stairs in the earth goddess costume, Ma asks me if I'm dressed as Peter Pan.

"No," Lou says. "She's a watermelon."

Then he lets out this real loud laugh from his stupid face.

At the S54 bus stop, Katie's dressed as a daisy, with a red bonnet buttoned around her head and a green leotard.

"Cool," she says. "You're a dragon."

"I'm an earth goddess," I tell her. "Get it right."

We walk to Chuck's house, which is in one of those little strips of white and blue town houses by the mall. Inside, they're playing some loud but slow trip-hop, and nobody hears us when Katie rings the bell.

I turn the knob. "It's open."

Inside is a long blue carpeted hallway crowded with a whole bunch

.ds who I don't know, probably students from CSI. And there's
essed as Cinderella smoking on the stairs and whispering to this
with misshapen teeth who's dressed as the Tin Man.

"Boy, it stinks in here," Katie says. "Like old socks."

And I can see Nicole in her roller skates and fishnets sliding toward us. Typically uncreative.

"No costume?" I ask.

"Clockwork Orange!" Nicole shouts over the music, pointing to her orange wig.

Then she drags us to this bucket of Kool-Aid full of floating eyeballs and fingers. She offers some to Katie, who declines. "No, I think I want a shot."

"Of what?" I ask. "Since when do you drink?

Katie looks at Nicole and sighs, then chugs a cup of the Kool-Aid and pours herself two Dixie cups of vodka. I pretend not to notice her rolling her eyes.

"Do you know where Alex Delvecchio is?" I ask Nicole.

And she points upstairs. "I'll go with you."

"Alex is the boy you like, isn't he?" Katie asks, extremely freaking loud.

Then I tell her to shush so Nicole won't hear.

The three of us have to push Cinderella out of the way to get up the stairs. The Tin Man tells us to go fuck ourselves.

"Ugh. That dude is like thirty-three," Nicole says.

Upstairs, there's a crowd of other characters: vampires and zombies and elves. Nicole pushes open a door, and there's Chuck and Alex Delvecchio sitting cross-legged smoking on the floor.

"Ladies," Chuck says, opening his arms. "Come. Sit down. Let's play a game."

He lifts a half full bottle of beer and pours the rest of into a small trash can underneath this desk. Then he spins it.

"Oh no," Nicole says. "I am not participating." She makes a quick exit. So that it's now only me, Katie, Chuck, and Alex Delvecchio.

"I'll play," Katie says. She sits down and unties her bonnet.

Alex Delvecchio looks up at me and must see the way I'm like, No freaking way, because he pulls my hand. "Come, sit by me."

"I don't like this game. It's very immature," I say.

But Katie's already spinning the bottle, and, just my luck, who does it land on but Alex Delvecchio.

Katie's palm slips slightly on a deck of cards as she crawls over to Alex Delvecchio and kisses his chin. Closing his eyes, he grins, pushes a finger in her armpit, then sticks his tongue in her mouth.

Let's pause here for a second right now. Imagine a piece of melon being scooped away from its shell. Imagine squeezing that ball of melon in your hands until the juice drips on the rug. That is my heart.

I want to tell Alex Delvecchio to stop. This is not the way it's supposed to be. She doesn't love you the way I love you, I want to tell him. She's Sleeping Beauty, and I'm Mulan. She's dressed as a daisy. Look, I am a god. She has a boyfriend named Robby, and during biology, they draw hearts on each other's binders. It would be enough to make you freaking sick. For Valentine's Day, he even bought her a two-dollar rose from the Our Lady of Hope and Mercy PTA and left it on her desk. Sometimes, when her parents aren't home, she gives him head.

Katie closes her eyes now, looking sleepy. Alex Delvecchio's closed his eyes too.

I can remember in sixth grade how Katie and I used to practice this exact same expression in the bathroom mirror. Afterwards, we'd play Bloody Mary. I'd turn off the light and have to cover the switch with my palm because she'd scratch at the wall, looking to turn it back on. I'd knock her hand away. "Bloody Mary!"

"No," Katie'd squeal in the dark, bumping her forehead into my lip. When she'd pull away, her bangs would get caught in my braces. And we'd have to separate our faces slowly. Afterwards, I'd pick her long hair away from the metal stuck on my teeth.

Katie makes a noise now like when we hum the scales out during choir—

a low D flat—and Alex Delvecchio's squinting as if he is trying to figure out the inside of her mouth, slowly.

I get up from the rug and search for the bathroom, where there's a green stain smudged on the tub, little bits of tiny hairs stuck on the sink, I'm assuming from Chuck's face, and a glass cup holding three toothbrushes, the ends of them sunken in shallow gray water.

I don't want to even look at the toilet.

In the mirror, my own face is white and puffy like my mom's, and like my grandma's and like my brother's. I'm not afraid. I turn off the lights. I say it three times. Bloody Mary. And afterwards, just like I expected, the only face in the mirror is my own.

When I get back outside, Alex Delvecchio and Katie have stopped kissing.

All three of them look up at me now. "Your turn," Chuck says.

Alex Delvecchio looks down at something in his fingernails, and Katie is chewing her gum now in wide circular gestures, staring distantly at the wall. They no longer look interested in each other. No longer in love. Because of course that's right, Arlene, I tell myself, it's only a game! Silly girl, I think.

"My turn." I kneel down carefully in my costume and sit on my heels. Then I spin it, praying to all the goddesses in the world that it will land on Alex Delvecchio. Not Chuck. Alex Delvecchio. Not Chuck.

Please?

But it doesn't. And when Chuck kisses me it's like he's eating my teeth, and his whole mouth is fast and wide. From the corner of my eye I can see that Katie and Alex Delvecchio are kissing again, but it looks as if she's fallen asleep. And then it is only Alex Delvecchio kissing her, pulling the top of her leotard down. Katie is there with her bonnet dangling around her neck.

I push Chuck's smelly mouth away. And reach out my arms to Katie. "Hey? Hey, freakazoid?"

She's not saying anything. But Alex Delvecchio turns around and looks at me and says, "Just chill."

Just *chill?* I don't *just chill.* "She's asleep, you creep."

"Man, get your fat ass away from me."

So I karate kick Alex Delvecchio's bootleg Skeet Ulrich self in the head, then yank Katie up from the floor.

He's cradling the place in his cheek where I kicked him.

"How's that for fat ass, huh?"

As I walk Katie down the stairs, she says, "You are my friend." She says, "Arlene, I love you."

The Tin Man is still hanging out on the bottom steps, his cardboard heart in his hands. "Leaving so soon?" he says. "What happened? You're not having fun?"

"I'm having fun," I tell him. "More fun than you."

"So, why don't you smile?"

"Don't tell me to smile."

"OK, OK, Penelope Pan," he says.

"I'll smile if I want to smile," I tell him.

"She'll smile," Katie murmurs into my shoulder, "if she wants to."

Do Now

Today, during class, when you wrote on the board, you tilted the chalk against the wall at an uncertain angle so that the lines you drew were barely visible: *Do Now: 5/18/10. Describe sugar for somebody who's never tasted it before.* And in cursive, too. The principal, who'd been sitting in the back of the classroom observing, noted it, the way the wall absorbed your voice every time you spoke, the way the fifth grade started to fidget in their seats, the sound of the chairs moving against the floor, pencils rolling off the desks, the students' whispers. Later, after school, in the office, he says, "That happens sometimes with new teachers, Miranda. Not being able to understand how they are seen or heard." He crosses his legs.

You look at the degrees on his wall. Amherst. Harvard. A portrait of him sitting on a rock in Thailand, his tiny, wiry frame folded over, elbow upon knee. And nod your head, trying to look humble and smart. You remember how once while staying late to submit quarterly student evaluations, you stood up from the desk, stretched your arms behind your neck, and walked down to the soda machine outside the teachers' lounge, where you overheard the principal talking about how stupid you are to the fourth-grade science teacher, a short, redheaded runner from Boston who's planning to quit in two years and apply to law school. This is the same woman who slowly smiles at you in the mirror over the sink in the bathroom while asking, "How you doing today?"

She laughed with the principal.

Now he sits in the office in front of you and smiles. "Teaching," he says, "is performance."

There's something about his face that you would like to break in half. Something which you would like to disassemble. When you drink with friends and they get tired of hearing you tell the same stories about your kids ("Damn, girl, you're twenty-three years old! Stop talking about work."), you often break off from the conversation, stare into a corner of the bar, and imagine the principal walking home at night alone: It is completely dark, except for a fast food–joint sign that rattles with light. Three men approach the principal and ask him for all his money. And a basic helplessness flattens the smiling sides of his mouth.

You want him to feel that way. Surprised. And humiliated.

"Let's talk about today's Do Now." He reaches over the desk to turn on the fan, though it doesn't help. The air conditioner is broken, and the Department of Education is waiting to find the cheapest vendor to fix it.

In the past, you've explained to him that you designed the exercise in order to teach imagery, but in terms of explaining the prompt that day in class to the kids, he says, you struggled. "There are also issues in terms of how you visually cue the classroom. And many problems with this assignment. Because first, it's not concrete enough for fifth grade. Perhaps an interesting *idea*, but not well articulated."

And you struggle with keeping momentum. For example, you take too long at the board when the kids walk in the room. "You write the Do Now on the board while class is in session instead of writing it before the students show up." And as a result Alexander Moreno started whispering in the back, and you didn't turn around quickly enough to reprimand him, so the other students took that as permission to begin talking, too.

You are a shy woman!

In the past, you've ignored initial challenges from the students, and so, unchecked, the class turns quickly. He says, "There may also be an issue here with the consequences you set in the classroom."

That is, the children sense there are none.

And in the past you've expressed that you believe if you take the misbehaving child outside and talk to her earnestly and honestly, in a forgiving manner, that the behavior will stop.

When side conversations in the classroom increased (to an inappropriate volume) you didn't turn around from the board to correct it. This may also be because you were nervous about being observed and afraid of trying to correct the behavior and failing. When you did turn around, you smiled. But the principal noted a slight agitation because your lip began to twitch. A tic. A tell. You asked them. You pleaded. "Do you understand? Pretend you are describing sugar for somebody who's never tasted it before. OK?"

Then Katrina, with her black bangs and purple glasses, raised her hand in the back and said she didn't get it.

Forcing a smile, you tried again. "Can somebody else explain?"

But nobody raised their hand. And the summer heat seemed to overwhelm the room. Then Alexander jumped up from the seat and started to yell because a giant purple roach had crawled underneath his desk.

"The girl. What's her name?" the principal says. "Who sits next to him? Elena? Lena? Also stood on her seat."

You remember that moment. You remember being confused, looking up from the small book in your hands, the one you placed beneath your lesson plans, to hide the trembling. You remember realizing the roach was there and running to the corner where it scrambled.

Now you nod diplomatically at the principal in a way that admits you knew you fucked up. He smiles, sideways and knowingly. "You told Alexander and the girl—what's her name?—to sit down, but the language you used for redirection—what was it? 'Enough!'—was unsuccessful."

This part is true. You admit it. You lost control. You remember how the whole class stood on their seats.

Opened their mouths.

And screamed.

* * *

"Oh, Miranda," the principal calls from his desk as you exit the office.

You gingerly rewind your footsteps, poke your head back into the room.

He looks up from some paperwork, lifting his pen to tap the air as he speaks.

"Try using the trip to the aquarium as an incentive for the class."

* * *

On your way back home, sitting on the train, you imagine how silly you looked as you ran to the corner of the classroom and lost balance. As you lifted your foot to step on the roach. In some ways you try to erase that memory.

And revise it.

Maybe your students were actually impressed when the ugly thing died beneath your foot. Is it possible you looked scrappy? At that moment, you looked practical? Did Joseph, who must sit in the corner at his own table, Joseph who cringes at big noises, relate to you just then? Joseph who loves to kill bugs and lay their carcasses on the kickball field in order to show you their insides.

Are you going to think about it all night long, even though you're supposed to meet your girlfriends and have a good time? You are taking a packed 4 train all the way uptown. Half the financial district is standing on their tippy-toes preparing to lose balance and fall, in addition to the crowd who got on at Brooklyn. Somewhere in the car, a man has found enough room to play the violin. The sound of his arm moving quickly back and forth against the wires like a buzz saw.

Tabitha will be waiting on the corner of 8th Street and Broadway. It is late spring. And as you walk up the stairs from beneath the sidewalk, at first Tabitha will look like a silhouette against the hot early evening light.

She will open her arms to greet you, one hand holding a cup of lukewarm coffee, the other hand wiggling its fingers: "Oh, Miranda!"

She'll hug you and the sun will shift across her dark shoulders, a new tan line from the thin straps of her expensive purse. She'll step away from two thirteen-year-old boys dangerously pushing each other next to a steady line of traffic. One of them pretends to hop on the bumper of a bus.

Ignore them.

They are not your children.

And you are not in class.

* * *

When you find the spot that Tabitha has picked inside the bar, you notice the long row of women's legs crossed over the bar stools, the fourteen-dollar glasses of white wine, the way the sunlight streams in through its pretty glass windows, the little pots of flowers that hang from the ceiling as if they were chandeliers, the busboys who look like your dead father.

You slump into the darkest corner of the table. Tabitha drapes one long leg over her knee. And inside her wrist you can see her name fashionably tattooed in graffiti. Both of you pause over bread, dipping slices into an olive oil that is dotted with basil. She drenches hers.

The bartenders are from Venezuela and speak a quick Spanish that eclipses your own. The owner of the restaurant is Israeli, but a free New York daily says it's the best Italian spot in the city. This is the way now that the both of you eat, which would stun your teenage selves, who used to scrape quarters out of their asses to buy fifty-cent chicken wings every Friday night at a Chinese spot in Stapleton.

Tabitha makes more money than you now. She works in finance. You don't resent it. Often she buys you drinks and dinner when you don't have enough to eat, which is usually at the end of the month, after the rent check has been cashed and left you minus twenty bucks in your account.

You love the way she laughs. Perhaps 200 years from now, in another life, the both of you will end up husband and wife. But today you are just friends who grew up next to each other since the day you were born. Your mothers told you that you were cousins and you believed it till you were fifteen and could not find a family line to connect the two of you by blood. In college you wrote each other letters back and forth describing your friends and boyfriends, promising you would never end up like your mothers.

Tabitha can dance and you cannot, but you love to move at a club. And oftentimes you can fake the rhythm, and if everybody is drunk enough they believe it. You owe this girl the aspects of yourself which are showable and come alive at night. Beside her you often feel three-dimensional, no longer flattened by the long hours of teaching and looking presentable in front of the class. With her, you feel like there are pieces of your face which might change color underneath the light. However, you also know that the parts of yourself which you own, the parts which are truly you, are actually as black as the earth and absorb the sun. You keep on waiting for who you really are to wake up and grow. Every year you expect a change, you expect to realize the world the way Tabitha sees it, like something to be peeled and split open like an orange.

But in conversations, while she talks about the men she loves and the women she hates, you are only able to talk about your children. "In my class, I have this boy named Alexander," you say. "And he never listens to me."

Tabitha smiles wickedly over the brim of her glass of wine, which has stained the corners of her mouth. "Beat him. Beat that boy," she says. "Take off your belt and beat him, Miranda."

Both of you are already drunk. You pretend to laugh, but even beneath your laughter, you feel as if you are irredeemably wrong, as if your body is a puzzle piece with one side that the universe has bitten off. That's why Tabitha calls you *la llorona*. Crybaby. Because ever since you were fourteen, sitting in the parking lot by the highway with one of her boyfriends, you'd stop three-quarters into the blunt, bunch up your face as if it were a rag, and cry.

Why do you do this?

Show up after work, travel an hour and half into Manhattan from Staten Island to meet her, when you already knew that in the end you would feel fucked up and wrong. Even beneath the gracious way your conversation sprawls, there's always some invisible current of sadness. There's always some hidden mine. Something's going to make you feel bad later.

Pendeja, you'll say to yourself aloud on the train ride home, the way your grandmother used to say as she was cooking in her translucent *bata*, the pockets sagging with candy. Your mother just coming home from school, throwing her book bag on the floor. Something's going to remind you that the way the both of you are currently laughing will not last long.

But for now, you watch Tabitha shove another piece of bread into her mouth.

She says, "Listen, booboo, you're gonna have to make those kids fear you in order to teach them respect."

* * *

Do Now.

When you get home at two in the morning, prop your right heel on the front steps of your building and balance your purse upon your knee. Don't let the contents spill on the floor. Look for your keys. When an old granola bar breaks apart in your fist and the crumbs squeeze themselves underneath your nails, don't get angry.

Instead, think: *Where's the fucking keys?* And hope you find them, so you won't have to bang on the door and wake your mother.

The dog now will bark your name.

She misses you.

Go back to the step, prop your foot up, and concentrate on the keys. Try to remember what they feel like. Find them in a tiny pocket nestled between some credit cards. When you get in the apartment, push the dog away or else she will bite you. She is young and she does not know yet how to love. When she stops barking, if she sits, bend down and kiss her. Fill her bowl with water.

Turn on the lights, then shut them off when you hear from the furthest edge of your apartment your mother moan in her sleep.

Now look for the dog's neck in the dark. Put the leash on her and drag her outside down the steps. Make sure she does not eat glass. Make sure she does not eat rocks. Watch her crouch down to piss. And listen to a group of teenagers yell "Happy birthday!" across the street.

They are drunker than you and you are jealous of them.

Remember to breathe. Then drag the dog inside.

When you open the junk drawer in the kitchen to look for one of your mother's cigarettes, remind yourself that soon one day you will be old. Remember your lungs. Find an old pack beneath last month's coupons. Run to the bathroom before you change your mind. Don't stop when the dog nips at your ankles, trying to love you. Break the whole pack of cigarettes in half and throw them in the toilet, so that both you and your mother will no longer be able to find them. Flush quickly. Watch the tobacco stick to the sides of the toilet. Don't listen to the dog crying outside the door, pawing at the floor. Bend down and hold your face above the seat.

Afterwards, wash your face with your mother's shaving cream because there is no soap. Pull your hair back tight the way your grandmother used to do when you were a child. Then try to feel new before you go to bed.

At night dream about *la llorona*, her gray face stuck behind the trees. Her head snapping back as she howls. Your grandmother warning you, as a little girl, looking outside at the brilliant, tempting world: If you misbehave, one day she will find you.

And that will be the end.

* * *

Do Now: 5/25/10. pg. 35 in Johnson's Elementary School Reader — Metaphor

As the principal suggested, you use exercises from the textbook for future Do Nows in order to (a) provide an easy way to give concrete and clear assignments and (b) establish a routine inside the classroom, so that while students work on exercises you can control their energy when they first sit down. In turn, this will also provide you enough time to compose yourself, read the students' behavior, and then react accordingly.

As you scrawl the last letter on the board, Alexander raises his hand in the back and says: "This is boring."

The rest of the children echo him.

You redirect by saying: "I know this is boring, but what happens next will be much more interesting!"

"Instead of directly addressing Alexander's behavior," the principal says later, after school, in his office. "Did you see that Alexander was looking outside the window and waving at a friend, assignment untouched?"

No, you didn't see it, you'll lie.

In an effort to save money the school has not yet turned on the air conditioner, and the underneath of your arms dampens. The principal himself looks chilly and you are afraid that he might see you sweat. It is very possible that at this moment you will cry and the thought terrifies you.

You try to redirect your emotions by focusing your gaze on something neutral and calming: the marble floor, the desk, a red ceramic mug. But ultimately you'll think of your mother lying in bed, hands extended into the air as if she were a small child begging to be lifted from her crib.

"What's wrong, Miranda?"

You shift in your seat: "Oh, nothing." And rub your forehead and pretend that you are tired.

"You know, the trick to teaching," the principal says, "is reflection."

* * *

The next day during recess you try to talk to Alexander earnestly and honestly. You find him standing with his feet shoulder-length apart, knees slightly bent, arms extended in front of him, his hands dangling at the wrists.

"What you doing, Alex?" you say.

Although you already know that, in order to control his anger, the principal has him take yoga on Wednesdays.

"Meditating," he explains.

"Oh, that's interesting." You ask him, "Can you teach me?"

Arms still extended, the boy does not even turn his head when he tells you, "No."

* * *

Today when you arrive at the apartment, strange smells come from the kitchen, and when you follow them you find your mother standing by the stove. She's stirring something and the steam has turned her face pink. It is a strange image. For the past three years, every time you've come home, you've found her asleep in bed. For a second you smile, till—surprised by the sound of your keys—she turns around, and by the dopey way her eyelids droop above her pupils, you can tell that she's high.

She says, "I made us dinner."

And even though she is only fourteen years older than you, the loose gray hairs along the side of her face make her look like your grandmother. "Set the table?" she says.

Now that you are both grown up, sometimes she'll do this, pretend you are a family.

You take out the forks. The both of you will sit down, and even though she made the rice with too much water, you eat it. "Mom. This is pretty good."

But at night you won't be able to sleep, because the insides of your face will itch and flutter. You'll think about Alexander and the principal's lessons on classroom management. On discipline.

You'll remember being fourteen and your mother's first round of cancer, not being able to see it and her pointing toward the piece of her body where it laughed. She was tight-faced and had just finished beating you. And it seemed to you then that the cancer belonged there, a hidden monster with no face or personality, just in front of her heart.

* * *

This is how you take thirty-two fifth graders to Coney Island.

Before you leave the building, count each and every one of their heads, pass out their name tags, make sure each one of them has a bagged lunch and a signed permission slip, remember that each detail owns its own set of details, which are equally important and not to be forgotten.

Outside, as you exit the building, walk backward along the sidewalk so that you can watch the children move. Constantly remind them to stay in line. While waiting for the train, line them up along the furthest wall of the platform so they do not fall into the tracks. Remind them to hold each other's hands.

Talk to the parent chaperones. One of them is Joseph's mother, who always smiles kindly and offers to help you by standing at the back of the line. The other's Katrina's father, a cop, who looks distracted and angry. He'll lose his patience. "Stop talking," he'll yell at his daughter while you walk to the aquarium.

At the ticket booth, you stop the class again for a head count. "Against the wall," you say in your most authoritative voice, competing with the voices of 200 other people.

"I counted thirty-two," says Joseph's mother.

You nod, relieved, and enter the gates of the park. First you show the children the seals, which bump their black noses against the glass. Alexander says, "Their whiskers make them look like dogs."

The class imitates their barking.

Then you show them the octopuses, whose purple arms explode against the tank like stars. You explain the suction cups beneath their tentacles. How each octopus has a beak-like mouth between its arms, how first the octopus grabs its prey then pushes it in its mouth. As they listen to you, the children twist their faces, and you wish the principal could be there then to observe and note each attentive smile. Especially Alexander's.

Then you bring the children to the turtles and the snakes that live inside a deep dark cave. Inside the exhibit, the blackness stuns them.

"Whoooa!" the students say, excited by the dark.

They break out of their lines to run to each green, dimly-lit tank of turtles. They push each other and one of them falls and slides on his butt across the floor.

How quickly you lose control.

"Fifth grade!"

A turtle turns his head and stares at you with prehistoric eyes. And Joseph's mother helps round the children up outside. Line them up against the wall. Frantically, you count their faces over and over again, but only come up with thirty-one.

This is how you lose Alexander.

* * *

When the principal shows up at the aquarium, at first he will not look at you. And though he is a small man, all of his movements right now look violent with disdain, the way he flips open his cell phone and dials Alexander's parents. The way he scratches his pen along the incident report or nods his head when he talks to the cops. After bringing the students back to the school so they can be dismissed, you quickly return to the park by cab to help look for Alexander. "When was the last time you saw him?" the principal says. "Did you count the children before you brought them to the turtles?"

Everybody separates now to search the aquarium.

The boardwalk.

The beach.

Some now walk along the waves, wondering if the boy decided to swim. You cry as you wander through the darkening aquarium, looking for Alexander. Calling out his name.

* * *

But ultimately you are the one that finds him, standing alone in front of the octopus tank, staring behind its multiple arms.

When you yell his name (Alex!) he tries to bolt, but your legs and arms are longer than his and when you catch up with the boy, you grab his arm, then twist, until he turns and looks up, finally, in full attention.

You lower your face so that you are eye level with the child. "Where were you?"

Even in the dark you can see Alex's face wrinkle with fear, the blue glow of the water sliding against the boy's forehead. "What were you thinking? Why would you do this? Huh?"

You find yourself shouting until something recognizable surfaces upon his face. That is, it reminds you of your own as a young girl, standing inside the bathroom in front of the mirror as your mother banged against the locked door. She'd said, "So you want to cry? I'll give you something to cry about."

* * *

When you walk the boy back to the group, Alexander looks tired, and the principal bends down to hug him. You can see it but the principal can't, the way Alexander rolls his eyes. And when you get back to the school and the principal sits you down in the office, barely restraining his anger, you'll ask, "Mr. Beckett, did you notice how much Alexander hated it when you gathered him in your arms?"

* * *

Do Now.

Collect your things. Only take what's personal. Leave the books on teaching, all the articles on classroom management and discipline. You won't be coming back here.

As you stand on the train on your way to meet Tabitha, think about the whole uncontrollable world. The cells mushrooming inside of your mother. The fifteen-year-old boy wedging himself between the doors now in order to stall the train so a crowd of his friends can board. The conductor yelling, “Please step away from the closing doors!” over and over again.

How free you feel right now.

Underground, as you look out the window into the blackness of the tunnel.

Wonder what Alexander must have seen beyond the octopus’s arms.

Underneath the Water You Could Actually Hear Bells

On the way back to Jersey from my mom's I was telling Dan about fifth grade, about how, for elementary school, my parents sent me to St. Albans with a coupon they'd gotten in the Sunday paper for 25 percent off the tuition: Enroll two kids, the third one goes to school for free. "Ha, ha," he said, but without laughing, as we drove away from my mom's in Staten Island. Dan grew up in a house where they paid full price for everything.

St. Alban's was an all-black and Latino school except for a few Sri Lankan kids who were Buddhist and an Irish girl who practiced witchcraft. There, I'd had a desperate fifth-grade crush on a boy named Rakim who was dating this Puerto Rican girl, Maritza. She was the type of girl who never got hit with the rope when she jumped in during double Dutch, who knew every song on *CrazySexyCool*, and who I envy still to this day even though she works at the Rite Aid across from my mother's house.

"What exactly about her do you envy?" asked Dan, leaning over the steering wheel into the dark. In the fog that was swallowing the Goethals Bridge, we could not see much in front of us. And the smell of shit was seeping into the car from the factories as we drove over the water.

"Everything. Her whole life," I said. And then I avoided pointing out ours for comparison.

I told Dan how, during recess, Rakim would pretend to have sex with

Maritza in the bushes, making loud kissy noises by the rectory while secretly I watched, hidden from their view behind a statue of the Virgin Mary.

"You big creep," Dan said.

I had not known what sex was till much later in sixth grade, when I'd read an advice column in one of my mother's parent magazines, in the bathroom, while I was peeing.

Baffled from Buffalo had written: *Dear Ms. Mom, My daughter came up to me today and asked: "Does it hurt when Dad sticks his body parts into yours?"*

I sat there.

Baffled in the Bathroom.

I did not know yet that women had holes. In my head I pictured something that you might punch into a wall. Then I looked between my legs to identify some type of circle but couldn't find one.

During recess sometimes, I would stand there at the flagpole watching Rakim chase Maritza around the yard. After Maritza became tired, Rakim would hit her with a kickball and run away so that she would chase him. Afterwards, during religion class, Rakim would shout: "Hey, Beatrice, how come you got none of this?" Then he would point to my chest.

In fifth grade, I took this as a vague come-on. At least Rakim was looking, I thought. And while it hurt, I was also grateful for the attention. In my ten-year-old head, I fantasized that perhaps it was code for *I want you, Beatrice. I love you. Please.*

So for Valentine's Day that year, I stuck a poem in Rakim's desk. After lunch, when he found it, he showed it to Maritza, who shouted out to her crew: "Miren lo que ella puso en su libro." Then she read the poem aloud, right there in front of the whole fifth-grade class.

"Ahem: Dear Rakim." She flipped her braids. "Sometimes the snow comes down in June. Sometimes the sun goes 'round the moon. Just when I thought our chance had passed, you go and save the best for last. By Beatrice Maria Santiago." Maritza crumpled the letter and threw it at my chest. "You did not write that shit."

"Yeah, I did," I said. I even puffed out my little chest.

"No, that's Vanessa Williams, you thief!" Then Maritza started waving our *Blessed Is the Lord, Jesus Christ* textbook at my head. "Don't be chasing waterfalls, OK, you little puta."

Which I thought was pretty unfair, pointing out Vanessa Williams and then quoting TLC.

I looked at Rakim, who stood there chewing his gum with zero remorse.

And all of the love for him that I'd accumulated and watered since second grade evaporated at that moment. Just like that. I could not understand why I had ever loved this kid. Everything I'd imagined and hoped for between us had rotted and expired. All of sudden, I could smell the stink.

Just like you and me, I wanted to tell Dan, sitting here in this car or in a small room with just the sound of a TV blinking in front of us. Or eating at his parents' house, the way he'd roll his eyes sometimes when I'd speak, or when he would ask me to speak Spanish in front of his friends. All of this I could have mentioned. And also that I'd found his secret email account. *You left it open, you stupid fucker.*

But any of this, did I say?

No, I did not.

* * *

The first thing I did after I found Dan's secret email account was call Cordelia Woo, who I have loved and cherished since sixth grade more than any woman or man or sunset or high-paying job. In middle school, I pretended to admire the Disney T-shirts she'd gotten during her summer trips back home to China in order to make her my friend, because in sixth grade I had none.

We were two of three non-white kids in an accelerated class at IS 21. The accelerated class was called the Cheetahs, which was code for "white kids with overactive parents." The Cheetahs might have been the only white students in the whole entire school, and some of the teachers had the good-natured racist humor to nickname the other classes the Slugs.

(Of course, I'm exaggerating. There were other white kids there, too. A few Italians. Some were Russian. And a girl named Sabina from chorus, who was Algerian—so I wasn't sure if she actually counted as white?) The first day of sixth grade, I walked into homeroom very disappointed. I had wanted to enter a classroom full of twenty-two Rakim look-a-likes—but there was only one black boy named Phillip, and he sat in the back and wasn't the least interested in me.

During lunch, most of the time, I sat next to Cordelia Woo. Very rarely did either of us sit with the rest of our class. She would trade me pieces of the microwaved chicken from her free hot lunch in exchange for the peanut butter sandwich my mother had packed. Those days I thought free hot lunch was by far superior to peanut butter and bread. And Cordelia was trying to lose weight, because she was planning to audition for the Disney Channel in December at the Staten Island Mall. (I'm sure that somewhere in my body there is a good amount of residual free cafeteria chicken from 1994 still clinging to my hips that no amount of hours on the treadmill will ever be able to erase.)

Now, all these years later, I looked at the cellulite growing on my thigh as I balanced the phone between my cheek and shoulder. "But how do you know that he's cheating?" the grown-up Cordelia asked. "Just because he offered to take her out for coffee?"

"When's the last time that motherfucker paid for my coffee?" I asked. "Where's my free coffee, huh?"

"I'll get you a cup of free coffee," said Cordelia, which was of course impossible.

Cordelia lived in LA, hundreds of miles away from my apartment in carajo-land Jersey.

"What a liar you are, Woo."

I flipped through the channels and waited for these strips of wax to dry on my legs.

"Actually..." And here Cordelia paused for effect. "I'll be coming to

New York next week." She squealed and celebrated over the phone line privately in all of her Woo glory. I could picture her dancing in her apartment in LA.

I should have been excited, but secretly I wasn't. I was not excited at all.

I had not seen Little Woo in a couple of years, and the thought of seeing her again *woed* me. Not because I did not want to see her, but because I did not want to be seen.

"What do you mean?" I asked.

"I have an audition," she said. "For a new show." Something off Broadway, a musical about werewolves that wanted to be humans and humans that wanted to be wolves.

I invited her to stay at the house for a weekend, hoping she'd decline, but instead she said yes. Then I imagined a grown-up Woo dragging her suitcase into my home, which though enormous was still mostly unfurnished. Inside of it, every movement I made echoed, and all that extra space had the strange effect of making you feel like your insides were echoing, too. The yard was full of tiny clumps of dirt that Dan had hired somebody to dig up so that we could put down the new grass we'd bought on sale from Home Depot. It was a very white and very dark house, with sliding windows and ADT stickers and one couch and a three-foot television set with two hundred channels and one dining room table, because we could not afford much else. That is after we paid for the house and the future lawn and the extra parking spot for the second car so that Dan and I would not have to ride in the same one to work.

"I can't wait," I said, fumbling with one last strip of wax.

The central AC banged and shifted cold air into the room. Then I thought about the texts I'd found on Dan's phone and the pictures of random women that I had forgiven last year but was too embarrassed to tell Cordelia about.

The bottom of a stomach. The soft, fat inside of a thigh. A small black breast.

"I have so much to tell you," I said.

But then Cordelia had to run away to an appointment and then dinner and then after that a party. She was running late.

In the bathroom, after we hung up, I stood in the mirror looking at the white strips of wax dangling below my knees, my mummified calves.

Then I ripped all of the hair out of my legs.

* * *

In seventh grade, there was this crew of Irish girls who sat in the altos section of chorus. Their ringleader's name was Kelly, and during rehearsal, she'd pile layers of white powder on her face to hide the acne while the sopranos practiced "Seasons of Love." This other girl, Hannah, would just sit there smirking or nodding at everything that Kelly said. Hannah had a slow face that rarely changed expressions, and when talking to her you had the feeling that you were conversing with a ten-dollar plant.

The Irish girls vaguely hung out with a group of black girls in the alto section. Specifically, they were trying to get cool with this one girl, Corinne, who they thought was in a gang. Which, of course, was bullshit, because I knew Corinne. We went to the same church, and I knew that she lived in a town house with a pool and a backyard and that her father was a cop.

In an attempt to impress Corinne, though, in the cafeteria, Kelly shouted, "Why does Cordelia always smell so much like armpit?"

She said this loudly, across the room, and poor sixth-grade Woo, with her *Mickey Mouse Club* pocket book, shrank into her free hot lunch. (So sadistic that Kelly was. I'm sure that she's somewhere out there in the world torturing more people, perhaps working as a physical therapist or waxing bikini lines in some third-rate salon.)

So, I stood up on the table and pointed at one of the pockmarks on Kelly's chin. "That's why you look like Freddy Krueger," I said, partly to impress this little Honduran kid I liked who took ESL on Tuesdays with Woo. But mostly I said it to make Woo laugh, which, in fact, she did. She laughed a lot.

Eduardo, on the other hand, looked up at me, mortified.

I told this story in bed to Dan, and he said, "Oh, well, wasn't that very nice of you?"

He was always doing shit like that, trying to call people out on things they never meant. Dan had this sense of entitlement that made him think he was psychic.

"With you, nobody can ever just really talk," I said.

"Talk then."

"Cordelia is coming next week."

I grinned and inspected Dan's face for any signs of enthusiasm. Cordelia had been my maid of honor and managed to look prettier in all of the wedding pictures than I did. In one of them, a group photo that we took in front of a banquet hall in Staten Island with all the maids and groomsmen propped on a long series of stone steps, you could see Dan looking at Cordelia instead of me.

Dan turned around in bed and raised an eyebrow. He had the type of nose and jaw you might see in a Norman Rockwell painting. "Oh really," he said. "Why?"

And there was something about his face that looked so pleased, just then. I was tempted to mention his secret email account but decided to wait till Woo got there so that I could do the whole thing in a way that would most offend him: Jerry Springer-style, with an audience. I imagined throwing a sneaker at his head and then leaned over in the soft dark to pinch his pale, long cheek.

I whispered, "She's coming to take me out for coffee."

* * *

In seventh grade, the only thing in the world Cordelia Woo wanted to do was play Sarah in *Guys and Dolls*. In the hall, sometimes she'd practice the part where Sarah gets drunk and dunks her head inside of a fountain while reaching out for Marlon Brando.

When she would imitate this gesture, Cordelia would erase her Chinese accent and speak this hyper-American English from the 1950s. Then she would pretend to be Sarah when she lifted her head out of the fountain: "You wouldn't believe me, but underneath the water you could actually hear bells." Never mind that she had actually mixed up the words a little bit.

We loved Cordelia's new version of the line better. Once, she repeated it over and over again in the bathroom until this eighth grader who was hiding out in one of the stalls smoking said, "Man, shut the fuck up."

On audition day, the drama director, Mrs. Schwartz, squinted at Cordelia and then gave her another script to read for a part in Sarah's mission band.

Politely, Cordelia placed her Mickey Mouse pocketbook on the stage and pointed out the problem. How could she possibly read from another script when she didn't even know that script's lines?

Duh.

She had practiced for Sarah's part, not the stupid mission band, Cordelia explained. Diligently. And then, "You wouldn't believe me, but underneath the water you could actually hear bells!"

"Now, now," Mrs. Schwartz interrupted.

But it was no use. Cordelia would not stop until Schwartz finally let her sing "If I Were a Bell." And then she bolted it, summoning every bit of experience of joy in her twelve-year-old body.

In the end, Sarah's part went to the math teacher's daughter, and Mrs. Schwartz made Cordelia a Hot Box girl. And during the Christmas performance, I sat in the audience and cheered for Little Woo as she sang "Take Back Your Mink," her voice lost behind all of the other girls' voices.

"Take back your pearls," she sang, holding that last note longer than she should have when all the other back-up dancers had stopped. Perhaps on purpose?

Probably in that whole middle school auditorium, I was the only one who heard her.

* * *

Anyway, what the fuck did Mrs. Schwartz know? Look, here Cordelia was fifteen years later, playing the leading vampire in the number-one-rated TV show for teenage girls.

Even now, as Cordelia walked toward me in the airport, she seemed slightly vampiric, with her black trench coat and purple velvet dress, but like a super nice vampire who supported the human race by drinking squirrel blood.

In the car, Cordelia said, "Tell me more about this fucker."

I told her all of the embarrassing stuff first. Everything. The raunchy texts and then the pictures. About how the first time I found them, I forgave him.

"No way," Cordelia said as we pulled out of Newark. And then, "But why?"

You could tell that Woo would never let somebody betray her like that, and I wondered what about me had allowed that to happen.

"I guess I just wanted so desperately for it to work."

"What do you mean?" Woo looked equal parts mortified and amused, as if it was such a silly, stupid thing, what I had done. This stupid thing which was such a big part of me.

And I wished I hadn't said anything.

For a second, I wished Cordelia hadn't come.

On the highway, I looked for an exit as I tried to remember something good about Dan.

"Maybe ten years ago, they were trying to kick my mom out of her house. The landlord wanted to rent it out to these college kids for like twice the fucking rent. This was back when Dan was still in law school, before we even got married. I tell him about my mom, and we're sitting in this fake French restaurant on Broadway, and he's like absolutely not, that is *fucked* up. Next day, he rides up to the landlord's house and grins at the guy, pretending he's my mom's lawyer. And he just starts talking these circles around him, circles—I mean, that's just how Dan was—till the guy gives up. Even apologizes. 'For any trouble I've caused,' the guy says. And just like that Mom gets to stay in the house. Dan walks back to the car and is just sitting there grinning. And there's like this energy ringing between us. I feel so proud," I said. "I felt so fucking proud, Cordelia. And he says, 'See. That's what you get when you stick with me.' "

* * *

Instead of going home, we decided to go *home*.

We reversed the car and headed over the Goethals Bridge to Staten Island. We walked into a bar next to the ferry, where we tried to find somebody from our old middle school who we recognized.

And we did. This kid named Mike Scaparo, who'd taped a flower to my locker once in eighth grade and sniffed paint with his older brothers after church, but who I avoided because even then I was unpractical. Look, a nice boy I could have married after twelfth grade. Probably never would this boy cheat on me.

In Mike's yearbook once I had written that if I bumped into him ten years from now and he didn't recognize me, I would hit him with a bat. And now, fifteen years later, there he was, tall and slightly overweight, but still very much attractive. His whole face was quick and dark with laughter, and he kept on making these goofy faces every time the Nets made a shot. By the pretend jukebox I fantasized about us getting married and staying happily working class until I scurried to his side of the bar, my little black heart pounding, arms wide open. In the background, Cordelia was nodding her head vigorously in support.

"Mike," I said. "It's me." Smiling.

I looked back at Cordelia, who was giving me a trembling thumbs up.

Mike leaned down, touching me on the forehead with his Mets cap. "Who?"

"Bea. From chorus," I said. "Beatrice," shouting over the game on the sports channel.

But he did not recognize me.

And I did not hit him with a bat.

* * *

At the bar, Cordelia and I practiced the different things I would say to Dan when I got home. And then we decided to leave the car by the water and walk to my mother's house, where Ma was thrilled and asked Cordelia for her autograph before creaking her way upstairs to bed.

Then we sat in the kitchen and I called Dan, and then I hung up.

Then Cordelia called Dan from her new cell phone and pretended to be a telemarketer.

And then I called Dan, but had forgotten all the lines we'd rehearsed at the bar.

As soon as he picked up, I started to say the same things that I would usually say, until Cordelia heard me saying them and shook her head vigorously. I put him on speaker.

"Where are you?" Dan said. "Hello?"

We were covering our mouths as we laughed at the sound of his voice.

Cordelia scrawled on a take-out menu in big crayon: *None of your business, MothrfucKeeeeeeeeeeeeeeeeeer*.

She mouthed the words and then tried to grab the phone.

"At my mom's." I pushed Woo away, ignoring her as she shook her head.

"So, are you going to stay there or are you going to come home?" Dan asked.

Cordelia was violently waving her hands in the air.

"Hello? Beatrice," Dan said as the phone fragmented his voice.

I looked up at Cordelia now, who was standing on the sofa frantically flapping the other side of the menu over her head as if she were a little girl again dancing on stage, her face lit with exhaustion and fury.

Then I read aloud the word she'd scrawled in graffiti and decorated with flowers:

"No."

This One Kid Douglass Got Jumped

After a while the cops didn't like us hanging out after school at the ferry terminal because Yesenia and Toya started doing too much, shaking and spraying their bottles of soda at the boys who pretended to like them, while Eddie ordered french fries off the ninety-nine cent menu and I begged to please just have one. Meanwhile, the loudest of us would practice the words *bitch*, *motherfucker* in our fourteen-year-old mouths so that everybody would notice who we were trying to be. Then we'd chase one another around the terminal or smack the boys in the head with our book bags, music playing off our phones, earbuds dangling from our pockets, or we'd sit on the railings of the sloping ramps to the bus exits to smoke.

The cops, they had to think of something.

To stop us they used bullhorns at first, and if you stood in front of the Dairy Queen and weren't in line to buy anything they aimed the bullhorn at your face and shouted for you to leave, until it got worse.

This one kid, Douglass, got jumped at the terminal by the S74 ramp by some kids who teased him in computer class: tenth grader Ryan Rodriguez, white Allen (not the Spanish one), and Christopher Andrews, who used to be good until his brother got locked up. If anybody asks who jumped him, we didn't tell you, though. Outnumbered, Douglass pulled out a Taser from his book bag. The cops, who had come to stop the fight too late, drew their guns and aimed them at Douglass, who lifted his skinny wrists in the air, confused, until they arrested him. One of them, shaking from having to draw his weapon, said "How could you do something so stupid?"

The next week the cops found something new to do to us. Every day at 2:45 p.m. they blasted this alarm that was so loud we left the terminal in search of somewhere else warm to hang out, somewhere that we could hear ourselves.

You Are a Strange Imitation of a Woman

The AC broke overnight, so me and Dolores are sharing a fan between our attached desks. We're also sharing a bunch of data entry so that we can make Tuesday happy hour at Bruno's, although I'm not feeling super up to it because they weighed me at the gyno this morning, and I wanted to die. Going to the gynecologist always makes me wonder why anybody would want to fuck me, which is what I tell Dolores.

"Frances," she says from behind her computer. "You said that very loudly." Then she points at Carrie the office manager, who's flirting with the CEO by the soda machine.

I lean across our attached desks. I tell her, "Listen. Dolores. Who cares?"

"I care," she says, and then just like that turns back to her computer and starts typing.

"You care too much."

Every night Dolores cleans her desk with a wet wipe, then tilts the keypad toward the floor so she can spray the crumbs away with a can of air—this for a bunch of people who don't even look at her when they walk into the room. Don't even say good morning, which is what I've been trying to explain to Dolores without sounding ungrateful because she got me this job two months ago and I don't want her to think I hate it. Even though I do.

But I will not let Dolores be duped. It is important that she discover the truth.

"How long have you been working here?" I ask.

"A long time, Frances," she says, not bothering to look up, her plastic nails click-clacking on the keyboard.

"But *how* long?"

Dolores stops typing and then counts. "Since before Adam," she says—Adam who is her son in kindergarten.

"And how much do you make?" I ask her, which is a dangerous question, I admit, but nonetheless necessary.

"Who cares?"

"I thought you cared. You're the one that cares. Aren't you?"

"It's none of your business," she says, even though already we've discussed her salary various times.

"I'm trying to make a point," I tell her.

"Are you?"

Now, whenever Dolores gets sarcastic, it makes me feel like the both of us are not very close at all. So I type loud and slow in order to make her laugh, but she doesn't. "Dolores, how old are we?"

She sits there quiet, and I slam my fist on our attached desks, making our shared cubicle tremble. "Thirty-seven, woman." I count from 1999 to 2010 on my fingers. "You've been working here eleven years, and you make about 3,000 more dollars than what you did when you started. That bitch," I point to Carrie, "is twenty-six, just started last year, and makes $15,000 more than you."

This is Carrie, who doesn't know how to use the fax machine or how to turn a document into a PDF or how to scan the invoices into the computer or even how to call the building manager so that we can use the freight elevator for deliveries. Although this woman is manager of the office, she does not actually know anything about managing the office, and everything she does not know she makes me and Dolores do.

"If you are so dissatisfied, Frances, you should consider finding a new job."

"You find me a new job," I tell her.

"I'm going to find you a husband."

"Find yourself a husband."

"I'll find us both husbands," she says.

"I don't want one." And for a moment, underneath the fluorescent light, I can't see Dolores's eyes behind her glasses. "You know what I've been thinking about lately?"

Dolores peeks at me from behind her computer. "What?"

"You and my brother Carlos," I say, because it's a thought I've been having for a long time—to hook up the two greatest people in my life and make the whole bunch of us family.

"Absolutely not," Dolores says.

"You could name that baby after me!" In my head I smash Carlos's and Dolores's faces together. I try to picture her long nose above his fat chin and them calling that poor girl Frances. "Frances, the Second."

"Lord no," Dolores says. "Stop it." But she's smiling and you can tell she's sort of considering it.

"Think about it—that's all I'm saying," I tell her.

Then she emails me an old invoice just to upset me, on purpose. "You formatted it wrong." Dolores points to the soda machine. "Carrie will be furious."

"Most likely," I say. "It doesn't take much."

Then I staple something loudly.

* * *

At Bruno's, Dolores will not go outside with me to smoke a cigarette. Because Adam has asthma, she says. She thinks the smoke will cling to her blouse. She thinks Adam will smell it tonight when Adam's father, Ralphy, drives up to the apartment and transfers Adam's sleeping body into her arms. She's scared Adam will wake up and start coughing. She's also trying to teach me a lesson. "You're too old to be acting like we're sixteen," she says. "Besides, it's hot."

So outside, I smoke alone.

And as a result this is what happens next: I'm standing there, minding my own business, and the skinny Dominican who works at the front desk at the building next to ours comes up to me and says, "What you doing out here alone... beautiful?" Which is the part that really upsets me—the way he says *beautiful* sort of as an afterthought.

Now, Tuesday happy hours are the only time Dolores can get Adam's father to take care of him for the night. Then after work, we can hobble to Bruno's to sit down, relax, and drink one three-dollar martini after another in order to understand the reality of things, how we really feel, aka the world. As a result, I'm not trying to hear nobody's bullshit—which is basically what it is, this guy coming up to me. I'm wearing a pair of size 10 JCPenney slacks from 2004, and I haven't even buttoned them. Because I can't. I'm a size 14.

So I tell this guy, who's got a face like a pit bull's, narrow eyes, and a wide mouth, "I know what I look like." Then I go inside and sit next to Dolores, who's texting Adam's father fiercely.

"Ralphy left Adam with his mother, instead of taking care of him his goddamn self," she says, then bangs the table with the cell phone.

Now, this is a common problem that Dolores has. Even if somebody else is taking care of Adam, all she can think about *is* Adam. And I've known Adam's father Ralphy since all three of us were kids, smoking on top of Dolores's roof, looking at the rest of Brooklyn. And Ralphy's mother is a nice old Puerto Rican lady who feeds you and feeds you and feeds you—much more reliable than Ralphy, who's thirty-six and smokes weed like he's still fourteen. So, to me, the grandmother's a much better babysitter.

But I don't tell Dolores this, because I understand that when you got a son and you take care of him with every inch of your day, and the father don't do shit, you have a right to be upset, even if those things don't make sense to be upset about.

"From the very beginning." Dolores stabs the table with her pointer finger. "The very beginning."

I shrug and nod at the same time. "Every year it gets harder for me to love somebody new!"

Dolores shakes her head as if I don't get it. "Me, I'm simple. I love the same people I've loved my whole life."

* * *

Back home at the apartment, I throw my purse on the floor and run through the hallway to Carlos's room quietly. Very quietly, I open the door. At this time of night, he's only a crumpled mountain of blue sheet snoring. A soft, fuzzy blanket of man. Behind the bed, through the window, you can see cars splash through the wet street, filling the room with the sound of them braking and then accelerating again.

"Carlos," I say, until he sits up and raises a fist in the air as if he were about to fight off an intruder.

"Jesus, Frances."

"Jesus, you," I say. "Jesus, Jesus!" I punch the air, then run to the bed and try to grab his fat face, but Carlos pushes me away.

"Go," he says, pointing to the door.

"I want to talk to you. I have an idea," I say.

But then he springs up from the bed and manhandles me out the room, sort of like *Bam! Fuck Frances*. Just like that. A game of push my old ass out the door. I smack him on the back of his gleaming head, my poor little brother, thirty-four years old, already going bald. "What's the matter with you?"

He rubs the part of his head that I struck to show me how much it hurts.

"See," I say, "that's what you get."

"Out, Frances. Out." He blocks the door.

"Little brother," I tell him. "I am not a dog. I am not some puppy. You cannot just shoo me away."

I shove him so I can get back into the room, but Carlos has always been so much stronger than me. Even when we were little kids. That boy was born big. The doctors had to pry his big cranium from between my mom's legs. So when Carlos pushes me, I slide out of the room, which makes it necessary for me to strategize. I know if I put my arm against the doorframe, he won't close the door on it because we're both grown-ups, and we haven't seriously hit each other since we were kids.

"Please, Frances. I'm really tired and you're really drunk," he says, which hurts.

"I'm trying to make a point."

Carlos sighs and opens the door so I can come in. He turns on the light and points to an old wicker chair from the Salvation Army, a heavy-ass chair that I dragged home down Bay Street for him last year, all by myself. "Go ahead."

So I sit. I touch a part of my leg where the pants feel like they're about to rip. Through the slacks I can feel some new piece of cellulite growing beneath the skin. Carlos is sitting on the bed, his hands sliding down his forehead, his eyes, his chin, leaving a trail of fingerprints where blood has rushed to the surface.

"I've been thinking about you and Dolores. I was thinking maybe you call her and ask her out for a drink."

"Why?"

"As a personal favor to me, your only oldest sister," I say.

Carlos lies down and turns his back to me, but I can tell he's sort of considering it, the same way that Dolores was sort of considering it at the office. "Can I go to sleep now? Can I go to sleep now, Frances?"

"Sure!" I tell him.

Then Carlos calls out suddenly from the bed, "Frances, you took your meds, right?"

"How kind it is, little brother, for you to think about my health." This kid!

Carlos sits up in bed now angrily, even though two seconds ago he was so tired. Now, the man is animated. "Frances!"

"You're shouting."

"Frances!"

"I don't respond to shouting."

"Did you take your meds?"

"Yes. I took them. Of course," I tell him, even though it's not true, because that stuff turns your brain into a sponge and the pills are more fattening than a box of donuts. And this year, I don't care, I'm going to lose twenty-five pounds—fuck lithium. I get up from the chair and try to make a quick exit out the room. "Dream about her," I tell him.

"What?"

"Dream about Dolores."

* * *

To convince Carlos is easy. Dolores is the one who's going to be the pain in the ass. In the morning, I look at her, this woman I've known all my life, trying to figure out how to convince her to fall in love with Carlos.

Dolores has always been about status. Even if it was just some boys in middle school and the whole bunch of us were broke, she'd look at them like whoever was the loudest or whoever could fuck someone up the most, *that* was the kid she loved. Even looking at Ralphy, you can sort of see it—the same pattern. After all, he was the funniest kid in school, and nobody was ever able to put him down without Ralphy verbally laying that kid out. In any case, Dolores likes her guys to be really good at something. No matter what it is.

"Carlos was almost a doctor," I say, because in college, before he dropped out, he'd been pre-med.

"Carlos is a cop," Dolores says, munching on something orange and delicious looking packaged in a loud crinkly bag.

"Yes, Dolores. Carlos is a cop. But he was almost going to be a doctor."

"Then why didn't he become a doctor?"

"That's not the point," I say.

"What is the point?"

Then Carrie passes by, and we become mum, like female robots, which Dolores is the best at. You should see that woman frowning while she examines a receipt. When Carrie disappears into the elevator, me and Dolores simultaneously put down whatever paperwork we were staring at. Then it's back to the point, which was: "Carlos is a smart guy, and he's got a lot to offer."

Dolores says nothing as the fan hiccups and rotates between us.

"Can I have one of your potato chips? Are those potato chips?" I ask.

"They're poison."

"Can I please have a piece of that orange poison, Dolores?"

She places the bag neatly on my desk. The print says *Gourmet*.

"These are expensive chips, Dolores. Where'd you get money like that for these pricey potatoes?"

She says nothing.

So I tell her, "I can see that I am getting nowhere with this conversation, which is unfortunate for you, because I am telling you right now that my brother is a catch." Then I look at her from behind my computer and stick out my tongue.

* * *

Because I am on a diet, for lunch I only smoke four cigarettes outside our building. I watch all the other secretaries and lawyers and bankers and big bosses sweat in Times Square. On the fourth cigarette, the Dominican from the bar last night comes up to me and asks if he can bum one. He's wearing a uniform, a blue blazer with too-long sleeves and a little gold badge that says *Miguel*.

"This is *my* lunch," I say, lifting the pack of Newports.

"Give me a cigarette, and I'll buy you lunch," he says.

"Take that lunch money and buy yourself a pack of cigarettes."

"Can I talk to you? I can't talk to you?" He looks at my dangling ID card. "I can't talk to you, Frances?"

"You can talk."

"Let me take you out somewhere nice," he says. "I know a nice place you'd really like."

My fourth cigarette is done, so I throw it on the sidewalk. A man in a blue suit holding yellow flowers runs up to Miguel's building. Immediately Miguel straightens his back, smiles at the man, and opens the door, letting the air conditioner blast between us. Once the guy is gone, Miguel slumps and shoves his hands into his pockets, looking from side to side as if itchy with a joke, the way boys used to do when they were young in a crowd, thinking of a way to make everyone laugh.

"So?" he says.

"So, what?" I tell him. "So, nothing."

"Think about it. That's all I'm saying."

Before I run across the street, back to work, I tell the Dominican no.

But you can sort of tell I'm considering it.

* * *

Further uptown, there's this fancy supermarket that Dolores likes to go to after work because nothing in that store is ever rotten and the cashiers there treat you with respect. I'm in the vegetable aisle looking at a box of expensive peppers, and skinny old Dolores is bent over the tomatoes frowning. She's got the Gucci purse she bought 33 percent off at Macy's dangling between her forearm and elbow, and she's sniffing the vegetables like a dachshund.

"Smile at the tomato, Dolores. You're getting permanent wrinkles."

"Fuck you," she says, bending over the tomatoes again as new veins bulge from the back of her knees like green fingers.

Outside, me and Dolores have to sprint in the rain to the subway before we go our separate ways. Then it's half an hour until she gets to Brooklyn. And at least an hour for me to reach the Island.

In the terminal, I keep away from the crazies camped out by the bathroom, where there's this meth head named Pam who likes to scream in the morning on the platform for the R train to "fucking come." Sometimes she'll sit next to random people in the terminal and introduce herself. "Hi, my name is Pam," she'll say, then slide down the bench to whoever-it-is until she's practically sitting on top of them.

She's standing by the bathroom now, asking people for cigarettes as everybody else crowds by the glass doors waiting for the boat to dock. When the doors slide open, we trample onto the boat like a herd and wait as the ferry glides across the Hudson.

At home, the apartment is humid and empty. It is a Wednesday, which means no Carlos till two in the morning. But there is evidence of him all around the kitchen. Dishes are drying on a piece of paper towel. Cereal boxes have been put away. He's tried again for the fifth time this week to scrub a round stain of wine from the table. The sponge he used and the stain are still damp.

In the living room, I balance a plate of day-old Chinese food on my lap while looking at the TV. Just looking at it. Never turning it on—I feel an overwhelming urge to talk. Maybe call Dolores. Though I have nothing to say. Besides, it's midnight, I think. Her and the kid are probably knocked out in bed. I'd wake them.

I wash the plate. Then I walk around the table until I get the idea to fall asleep.

In bed, I spend two hours blinking.

* * *

Turns out I should have called Dolores. She'd been awake all night taking care of Adam till one in the morning because of his asthma. When the inhaler didn't help, she called Ralphy, who was stuck working till three in the morning. She took a cab to Woodhull Hospital and waited two hours in the lobby with Adam, who'd fallen asleep on her lap by the time the doctor called her. "Pues, what the fuck. Why did I even come, you know? Ten dollars on a cab for nothing. That's why I hate the ER," she tells me on the phone as she runs to the train.

She's an hour late, and I'm typing up some of her invoices so she doesn't fall behind. But I have to hang up on her mid-sentence because Carrie comes by just then, clicking to our desks, then stops and stares at Dolores's empty seat.

"You need something?" I ask.

"Where's Dolores?" Carrie says, straightening her back, trying to sound authoritative in a way that almost makes me feel sorry for her. Like when I see her in the break room, sitting at one of the round tables alone, eating her yogurt quickly and staring at her phone, while all the other secretaries crowd in the corner and laugh at each other's jokes.

"In the bathroom," I tell her. "You need something?"

Then Carrie lifts her chin and walks away.

Twenty minutes later, it's Dolores running into the office.

"You were in the bathroom," I tell Dolores.

"Right." She untangles her purse from a Century 21 bag full of paperwork. "Boy. That Dominican *loves* you. He practically followed me upstairs." She wipes the sweat on her neck away with a Kleenex. "He was smoking outside when I came in, and then he was like, 'Hey, you're Frances's friend, right?' I said, 'Listen, guy, I'm late.' Then he opens the door for me and goes, 'Tell Frances I miss her.' "

"Oh, god."

"He's not bad looking." She wrestles with the computer to turn the modem on, then nods at Carrie's office. "What did I miss?"

"Nothing. She walked around the desk a couple of times and farted."

Dolores raises one hyper-arched eyebrow at the computer screen as it beeps ON. "I had to go all the way to Flatbush to drop Adam off with Ralphy's mom."

"Good choice," I say.

"What the fuck does that mean?"

"Better Ralphy's mom than Ralphy."

Dolores adjusts the fan.

"I gave the Dominican your number," she says, obviously just to piss me off.

"Why?"

"Because he likes you. What's wrong? If he was an asshole, you'd love him," she says, which is true. I'll give her that. I've always been like that with assholes: Look. Here I am. Love me, I'd say, since I was fourteen years old.

All of a sudden, Carrie pokes her head out of her office shouting, "Dolores!" Real loud, in front of everyone, to embarrass her on purpose. The other secretaries turn their heads toward our cubicle, ready for a show.

"Coming," Dolores says and then cringes. She's smoothing her skirt and wiping sweat away from the back of her neck.

"You were in the bathroom," I remind her.

But it's no use. Dolores does not know how to lie. So I stand up and tell Carrie, very professionally, "Listen. She was in the bathroom. Okay?"

Then Carrie gives me this look like, Who the fuck are you? So that I'm thinking, Wait, who am I, lady? Who am *I*? Who are *you*? Then little Miss Dolores turns around and looks at me sharply, putting her finger on her mouth, and tells me to shush. As if I wasn't the one defending her. As if I was the one who was wrong.

* * *

Outside, during lunch, I am accosted by the Dominican, who wordlessly offers me a cigarette.

"Great. I no longer own the privacy of my own lunch breaks," I say.

"You know, soon you're not going to be able to smoke out here. Bloomberg's going to ban smoking in public places."

"Fuck if I care."

"Oh, well. How are *you* today?" he asks as a string of cars honk behind him in unison.

"I heard my friend gave you my number. Stop accosting my friends," I shout over the noise.

"See, even your friend thinks we're a good idea."

"She has poor judgment. You should see the types of guys she thinks are good ideas."

Miguel squeezes out a thin line of smoke between his lips and begins to whistle an old Spanish song that sounds so familiar it feels like I've known it my whole life, except I can't remember what it's exactly about, only that some parts are about love and the rest of it is just some old sound I can't put words to.

When he stops whistling, I clap, like a good audience. "What else can you do?"

"Poems. Ballads. Sonnets," he says.

"Please."

"Really." He lifts his right hand. "I swear."

"Let's hear it then."

"I don't know. I don't think you're ready for it."

"Just go."

Then Miguel straightens his shoulders. "Ahem.... Fuck does Bloomberg care / About my public health and / Not when cops beat me." He grins. He bows.

"You're ridiculous."

"You like that?"

"Ridiculous," I say. "Stop bowing. It's embarrassing."

"That's a haiku," he says. "A haiku for Frances."

* * *

Upstairs, I tell Dolores that fine, she's won. I'm going out with the Dominican Saturday, to which she says, "Don't wear that shirt with the gold sequins."

On my way home, sitting outside on the boat, I inventory the piles of clothes in my closet: a couple of bridesmaid dresses, work pants, an old uniform from my former job at the pharmacy. Crazy Pam comes out just then, fighting as usual with this guy I nicknamed Skeletar once because his face looks like it's dripping away from his skull.

"I will eliminate you," he says to Pam. "I will shove you into the water. The flora and fauna will eat your brain."

One of the ferry workers, a skinny twenty-year-old red-faced kid, follows them as he radios the cops. Pam poses against the rail. "Do it. I dare you," she says.

The pitch in Skeletar's voice rises to that of a woman's now, and Pam is imitating him as one of the ferry cops coaxes her off the rail. I stay looking at them through a pair of sunglasses, so that they can't tell.

Sometimes I just like to hear the both of them scream.

* * *

Saturday, Carlos pokes his nosy head in my room. "What's happening in here, *viejita*? You moving out? Why you got clothes all over the floor?"

"I've got a date," I tell him.

"Ho ho ho," Carlos says.

"Is it that hard for you to believe, little brother, that I am a desirable woman?"

He sits on my bed holding a whole bag of barbecue chips and puts a two-liter bottle of soda on the floor. "Not at all."

In the mirror, my *chichos* bloom over the top of my jeans. From the back of the closet, I pull out a blouse with all these gold sequins.

"Oh, dear," Carlos says.

"What?"

"That shirt just gave me a headache."

"This?" I ask him. "This is *nice*. Your problem is you have no taste."

"Please." He stretches out on the bed. "You got that shit 20 percent off at Bang Bang," he says, crunching a handful of chips.

"Can you go?" I tell him. "You can't *go*? You're stinking up my room and I need to concentrate on tweezing my eyebrows."

"Ho ho ho," says Carlos. "Excuse me, Miss Thang." On purpose, he stands and swipes the crumbs off his sweats onto the bed.

"I could hurt you."

"Just not too much makeup," he says.

I lower the tweezers and look at his reflection in the mirror. "What do you mean, not too much makeup?"

"You just have a habit of putting on too much makeup, and then it makes your whole face look, you know, kind of crummy."

"Crummy?" I tell him. "You need to get your fat ass out of my room. That's what you need to do."

"Like a peacock," he says as he exits. "A forty-year-old peacock."

"I'm thirty-seven," I shout as Carlos bangs the door shut.

* * *

On my way to meet Miguel, there's this European family on the ferry. We're all sitting on the deck, and the father's giving the kids bread so they can feed the seagulls. One aggressive bird keeps swooping down, almost biting the three-year-old. And the mother's saying something angry to the father in some type of Scandinavian language that sounds like, "What the fuck—you let the three-year-old feed the seagulls?"

I'm sitting there watching the woman curse her husband out when, all of a sudden, I hear, "Hey. Thanks for saving this seat for me." The voice crackling like a crumpled paper bag.

I look up, and it's Pam, wearing twenty different types of plastic bracelets like she's fifteen years old and going to a rave. So I pick my purse up, then shuffle along the bench closer to the tourists, hoping that she'll bother them instead of me. I even sort of point at the father and wink at her.

Instead, Pam slides down the bench until her thighs touch mine. "Let me tell you something, lady." She leans over and touches the sequins of my shirt as if she were petting a snake. "You are a strange imitation of a woman." One of her nails snags briefly on the edge of the blouse.

"Don't touch me," I say, moving down again a few feet.

"So, you're too good to sit next to me, huh?" she says.

"Not at all. I just wanted to give you a little room."

Pam stands up and walks over. "I didn't ask for no room."

Which puts me at a predicament, because I can no longer ignore her.

"You deaf?" she says, startling the family of tourists feeding the seagulls. The mother pulls one of her babies toward her.

Then Pam grabs my hand, pushing her thumb into the forearm, squeezing. I stand up and tell her: "Bitch, you want to box?"

Then she lunges forward.

But I push her, just in time, so that she falls on this man, spilling his coffee all over the floor. I tell her, "I'm fifteen types of crazy, lady. Just try me."

Pam stands up and grins, her face lit like a white jack-o-lantern. "Do it again."

Everyone on the boat is watching us now, and not one of them is a cop, which is real fucking convenient. Black kid from the Bronx leaves his apartment at night, there's five cops waiting to check to see if he has his ID, what he's doing on such and such block, if it is true, in fact, that he has weed in his pocket. Meth head jumps me on the boat, and not a single one of them is around.

"Stay away from me." I put my hand out. "Pam. I'm serious."

"You wait till we get off this boat," she says.

"I'm serious," I tell her, walking backwards slowly till she turns away.

Outside, I sit on the other side of the boat and watch the beginning of Manhattan, the different dark pieces of Battery Park. Every now and then, when someone opens the door to sit outside, I can hear Pam still talking to herself about the things she wants to do to me.

* * *

The last time a guy took me out was a year ago—Frank from Brooklyn, this half-Lebanese, half-Italian guy from Bensonhurst who I'd been seeing for a couple of months until his wife Nicole called me on his cell phone, asking if I knew that he was married.

"Yes, Nicole, I know that Frank is married," I said. I was using the house phone in the living room, so Carlos heard me. When he poked his head out from the kitchen, I put Nicole on speaker. "So that you can better hear, Mr. Nosy."

Then the lady went crazy, telling me about what she was going to do if she ever found me talking to him again and about how Frank was *hers*. She said, "He belongs to me!"

"Nobody belongs to anybody," I said, and then I hung up.

Still, that night I went to bed feeling fucked up, and in the morning I called Frank and I told him, "I don't think I want to see you anymore."

For a little bit, I was proud of myself. I quit smoking. I bought everything diet. Me and Carlos started going on walks at night sometimes before he started the late shift, and he would tell me all about the other guys at work and then about a girl they picked up off the street for selling herself. Afterwards, they drove her back to the precinct, where she called her father crying, asking him if he would let her come home. But the father said no.

These things hurt my brother too deeply.

Walking with Carlos along Bay Street, seeing all the dead buildings blend in with the trees, hearing about that girl at the precinct, I told him, "You're a good person." And I went to bed thinking I am becoming the woman that other people want me to be. But when Saturday came along, and I didn't have anyone to be with, I couldn't help thinking about Frank, how he would always have a woman on the side, and how his wife would always be angry and hurt. So really I had done nothing to rectify the situation. Nothing had been changed. And if Frank was still going to see other women, and if Nicole was still always going to be unhappy, then I might as well have stayed with Frank, instead of sitting in my living room all alone on the weekend.

So, I called him. I left a message, and when he didn't call me back the next day, I dialed over and over again, twice an hour until eight o'clock.

But he never picked up.

* * *

The menu has no prices. It is a restaurant on the West Side, and when I go inside Miguel is sitting at the table looking very pleased with himself, like: Here. I told you I knew a good spot. It's a restaurant I could imagine Carrie going to, sipping wine while sending passive-aggressive emails to the bunch of us on her Blackberry. At the table next to us, a woman speaks loudly about her daughter's "adventures" at Princeton and then laughs as if she were singing opera. The waitress is slow to take our order, and Miguel pretends not to notice when she ignores him after he opens his mouth to stop her.

We talk about other things: where he lives in the Bronx and where I live on the Island and each of our long commutes. The 1 train. The 6. Walking home at night. I say things about the boat.

"You live alone?" he asks.

"I live with my brother."

"Older or younger?"

"Younger. Only a few years, though."

"You don't get tired of that?"

"Never," I tell him. "We've always taken care of each other. When we were growing up my father would try to kick my ass, and Carlos would get elaborate about distracting him. My dad would be like: 'What the fuck? Where have you been, Frances?' And Carlos would be like, 'Look, Dad. A comet!' "

"I could see you being a bad girl," he says.

And this makes me cringe. Here I am saying something about my brother. Here I am saying something about myself. And there he is being slightly repulsive and corny.

"I hate this restaurant."

"This is one of the best restaurants in New York. What? You didn't know?"

"It's expensive for no reason."

"It's not expensive at all."

"They must pay you a lot to open doors," I say.

And for a second he looks like he might toss his very empty glass at me, and I think, Go ahead. Let's get to the bottom of what this will finally be about. But instead he's like, "Cool, so you'll understand if we split the check?"

"You better get ready to wash some dishes."

"Why are you fighting me?" he says. "Why are you fighting me? Relax."

"I am relaxed," I say as the woman next to us *ha ha*'s even louder. "Though I really don't even know why I'm here."

Miguel stands up, tossing his napkin, like he's the leading chick in a novella. "Fine, then. Let's go," he says, so that the woman stops laughing now and looks at him as if he were about to snatch her pearls.

When we pass by the waitress who never gave us water, I say, so that all the other customers hear it, "How come a nice, fancy place like this has roaches?"

Outside, I turn left on Broadway toward the 1 train.

Miguel catches up with me and asks, "Where are you going, huh?"

I point to the subway, but he blocks me.

"No," he says. "Come."

* * *

The whole time on the D train, I can smell myself sweat. I remember doing things like this as a teenager, following men I barely knew just because they said, "Come."

We end up at a cheap Mexican restaurant, where I order a neon pink margarita the size of my head. I order one after another. Then we walk to Miguel's building, which is all fucked up inside, bright green and orange and blue, almost like a Rubik's Cube. Walking up a set of peeling stairs,

I predict his apartment will be equally hideous. But when he opens the door, all you can see are pictures: huge black-and-white photographs of trees, sparkling gray bodies of water, giant happy wrinkled faces, black and silver rainbows. "I took these," he says.

On one wall, there is a series of long windows with glossy plants sitting on their sills, some buried in large red pots, some hanging on hooks from the ceiling. He moves to the kitchen and turns on the faucet. "You want some water?"

I reach into my purse and throw one receipt after another on the floor until I find my phone to text Carlos. I let him know I'm going to stay in the Bronx, so that he won't worry when he comes home in the morning and doesn't see me around. And do you know what that knucklehead has the nerve to write back?

Ha ha. Old woman. Have fun.

* * *

Monday afternoon, Dolores is delighted. "Love," she says, "is a good thing."

"I can see that," I tell her, polishing my screen and tweezing the crumbs out from the keyboard. "Which is also why I think you should talk to my brother."

Dolores groans.

"Imagine," I say. "You two get married. Combine your finances. Move into a nice little town house in Tottenville. Your kids grow up talking like guidos."

"No."

"Christmases, you decorate the windows with those little easy-to-peel-off decorations of snowmen and reindeer. Carlos is in the kitchen, burning the ham. Probably sneaking pieces of it into his chubby, chubby mouth. You know, the way your mom makes the ham with the pineapple. You're pregnant and screaming at me for smoking while me and Adam laugh, because you're too slow and fat to spank Adam."

"I love Ralphy."

"You have two cars. Carlos makes you quit this stupid job, and you stay home and crochet and watch TV all day, rubbing your belly like a hungry, hungry hippo."

"I love him," she says, which is the truth, I guess, but that does not mean I have to like it.

Carrie walks by then and flicks a stack of invoices on my desk. "You formatted them wrong," she says, tapping a finger on my computer screen. "So?" Tap. Tap.

So?

There are many things I would like to tell this woman, like for example if this were any other place, if this were not an office, if I weren't broke and if she hadn't managed to be my boss, and if she was just some little piece of shit *blanquita* riding the train in her overpriced outfit, I bet she wouldn't talk to me like that. I bet she wouldn't say shit. But instead I pick up the invoices gently and put them beside the computer. I try to focus on some concrete action, which will make me look professional and calm. For example, I think about the list of emails I have to send out today. Then I think, Just look at the bitch, Frances. Smile.

"I'm talking to you," Carrie says.

"And I don't appreciate the way you're talking to me," I say right back, which upsets Dolores, of course.

She stands up between us, with one hand out. "Frances."

"What?" I tell her.

"Frances!"

"Yes, that is my name."

Then Carrie, twisting her face in six different directions, has the nerve to turn around and tell me, "Go home. Now." Just like that.

So, fine. I go home.

But before I leave, I tell Carrie to go fuck herself, so that all the other secretaries turn around. Poor old Dolores is so nervous that she is meaninglessly moving stacks of papers back and forth on her desk, from the stapler to the computer, back to the stapler again. And Carrie is trying to dial security before I leave the office, so that they'll escort me out of the building.

But I've beaten her out the front glass doors before she's even hung up. And I can hear her now asking one of the secretaries: "What are you looking at?" And I'm pressing the button to the elevator before security comes up. I'm pressing the button so that the doors will open. When inside the elevator finally, I can feel my body humming some loud, quick song.

* * *

Outside a man clips the edge of a cab with his bike and beats the car's roof with his hand as steam lifts away from the street and circles his bare legs. I push through the rotating doors of Miguel's building and ask the bald Italian guard at the front desk, "Where's Miguel?"

"He doesn't work today," the guard says, looking up briefly from his paper, then looking back down.

Outside, I dial Miguel's number over and over again, but he doesn't pick up.

* * *

First, I go to Bruno's and drink a couple of beers. I tell the bartender, pointing to a couple of characters slumped at the end of the bar, "Nobody better sit next to me. None of them."

Then on the way back to the apartment, I lose my keys, and I have to bang on the door until Carlos hears me. He answers it shirtless because of the heat, with his stomach hanging out over his jeans.

"How come every time I open the door, you're drunk?" he says.

"Don't be mean to me tonight."

Inside the kitchen, he gives me half the meatball hero he ordered. A piece of cheese dangles from his lip. "So, what happened?"

"They fired me."

And though Carlos tries to hide it, I know that he's thinking about the rent and how I've gotten fired from my last two jobs and all of our numerous combined debts. "What happened, Frances?" he says gently, still trying to be on my side.

"They fired me, *Carlos*," I say, a little bit nastily. I know he's trying to be patient, but I hate how he automatically assumes it's my fault.

"Why?"

"I got into a fight with the office manager. She threw some shit on my desk, so I blew up a little bit. And that's it. She told me to go the fuck home."

Carlos opens a cabinet door then slams it. "Jesus," he says. He walks to the living room and turns on the TV. Then turns it off. "Jesus, Frances."

I squeeze both parts of the hero together so that the meatball and sauce splatter on the plate. "It wasn't my fault." I had tried. I had wanted things to work out.

Carlos walks back into the kitchen and starts washing the pile of dishes I left there from this morning. "How are we going to make rent?"

"I'll find another job. It's not that big of a deal," I tell him. And then playfully, "Stop having a titty attack, okay?" When he turns around, I point at his chest. "See, when you get upset, your boobs tremble."

"How the fuck are you going to get a job?" he says. "Dolores was the one that got you that job."

Which is truly offensive, but I understand that Carlos is mad and that he needs to say these things, so I stay quiet before I say something I don't mean.

"All I ask is you help out with the rent. Shit, all I ask is for you to pay the electricity. And then it's like you don't even care. I'm busting my ass. I work all night this shit job and you decide to mouth off and get fired." He opens the cabinet again and pulls out my pills. "You haven't been taking them and don't say that you are because I know you're not." Carlos opens the bottle and places a pill on the table. "Take it," he says, which was the way my dad used to do growing up, except the words and the movement are comical coming from Carlos.

I stand up to make my way out the kitchen, but he blocks the entrance. "No," I say.

"Take it."

"I said fucking no, Carlos. You don't tell me what to do." And then I laugh at him, because at this moment he deserves to be laughed at. "You know nothing."

"I know nothing," he says.

"You know nothing."

"I know nothing," he says, quietly. "I'm the one who's always taking care of your ass, and I'm the one that knows nothing."

All of me feels shrill, like a box of broken glass. "I took care of *you*, Carlos. Since I was thirteen years old. Who got up in the morning and fed your ass? Who walked you to school? And who the fuck are you? You loser. You obese slob with your shit job. Who are you to judge me?" I push him.

Then Carlos grabs my face and drags me to the table. I keep punching him on the side of his cheek until he gets hold of my hair, twisting it with one fist. Both my hands spring to my head. Maybe Carlos gets scared. Maybe Carlos feels bad because suddenly his fist becomes hesitant. The fingers loosen, and I turn around and swing at him until he fully lets go.

Free now, I swipe all of the fucking dishes on the floor. Then Carlos comes behind me and squeezes my face again with one hand, the other arm wrapped around my middle. We pause here, stuck like this, unable to move, sweating, until his fingers grope across the table to pick up one of the pills, which he shoves between my lips. "I swear to god, Frances. Swallow."

At first the pill feels like nothing on my tongue, small and tasteless. But I know already the deceitfulness of its size. "No," I tell him. It makes me feel dumb. It makes me feel fat.

When I spit the pill out, Carlos catches it and forces it back in my mouth, so that I'm looking at my baby brother who is no longer my baby brother, but a grown man, who's pinching my nose so that it has begun to bleed.

I bite the pill.

I tell myself as I do it that it does not make me a weaker person because

I swallow. There is no other choice. And if there's no other choice, I cannot be held responsible for this, which has nothing to do with me or who I am. Once the pill's gone, Carlos lets go of my face and bends down to pick up all of the dishes I have broken.

The naked fat slope of his young back makes my heart wrinkle like a blanket.

* * *

What has turned Carlos into this new ugly person? My beautiful brother. If I am the reason why, then maybe I have denied him many beautiful lives, ones in which he does not work from ten at night to six in the morning, ones in which he does not drag his sister by the hair into the kitchen.

At night, once Carlos leaves for work, I begin to pack some things. I fold all of my blouses neatly. Such organization is necessary for a new start. Then I wait outside for the bus and make my way to the ferry. Two in the morning, on the boat, I drag my suitcase onto the deck, where I'm the only one there except for Pam, who's leaning against the railing, whispering to herself through her crumbling teeth as the Island shrinks behind us.

We don't bother each other. She looks out at the water. I look out at the water. We watch the whole sparkling thing repeat itself until we reach the city.

The Grant Writer's Tale

The news notification blinged and popped up on all of our cell phones and Facebook feeds simultaneously: *Pantaleo: Not Indicted by a Staten Island Grand Jury.* All of my office mates were white, and though they had expressed polite concern in the past about police brutality (of course, making sure to qualify that concern with some apprehension about the vague details of Michael Brown's death and, well...his character), when the news slid into their timelines they all looked down at their phones at once, sighed ironically, x'ed the notification from the screen, and continued to finish whatever email or RFP they were very strategically wording. The sound of their fingers tapping at their keyboards all at once vibrated like a bunch of winged insects swarming. That year there had been a major deadline upon us, and all of our jobs depended on securing the grant. "By any means possible," Susan said, Susan the ED.

I began to sweat.

Susan liked to keep the heat at 74 in the office because her new juicing diet left her perpetually hungry and cold. During staff meetings the hot air dried out our throats, so that sometimes I'd open my mouth to begin a sentence and suddenly feel a tickle at the back of my tongue that would travel to my chest and send me to the water cooler in a fit of coughing. It had made me afraid to talk during meetings, so that I nodded at whatever anybody said. At the end of the meeting, I'd shuffle my notes into my folder and walk quietly back to my desk, the artificial taste of cherry cough drop stuck in my throat.

The video of Pantaleo killing Eric Garner shows this: Garner standing in front of the beauty supply store on Bay Street, next to Tompkinsville Park, telling the officers: "Every time you see me, you want to mess with me." Later, Pantaleo jumps on Garner's back and swings from his neck, bringing him to the ground with a choke hold. Four officers crowd Garner, who's collapsed on the sidewalk, as he repeats: "I can't breathe. I can't breathe. I can't breathe." Softly. Each word ticking in time like the pendulum of a metronome. His voice muffled by concrete.

"It doesn't make any sense." I scrolled down the newsfeed to try to find more articles about the grand jury decision.

Everything had been recorded. Everything was on video.

The program manager, Jeff, who sat in the adjacent cubicle, overheard me talking to myself and chuckled. "Come on, bro. I saw that coming a mile away." Then stood up and leaned over the gray divider to ask the ED, "So, Susan, what exactly do you want me to do with this budget? What are we looking at in terms of administrative fees?"

My hand hovered above the keyboard but started to shake. I waited for it to calm down, then capped the yellow marker I was using to copy edit a project narrative, clipped the pages of the proposal back in order, and filed it in the folder of applications for FY15. Once everything was clean I made my way through the gray and blue maze of cubicles toward the door to leave.

But when I passed the ED's desk, she looked up at me and lifted her pointer finger as if she were calling on a waiter: "Are you headed out for lunch, Luis?" Then she reached into her purse for her wallet. "Get me a cup of coffee, please?"

The fluorescent office light cut through the expensive foundation on her pinched face and lit up the very thin line of gray growing along the crooked part of her dyed brown hair. And the juice she drank at breakfast had stained the corners of her lips green.

When I had first started this job, I thought that Susan was someone very smart and clever who understood people well, who understood people more than they understood themselves. When I told my parents that I had gotten this job, my mother, who never went to college, never worked an office job, and certainly did not fully understand what a grant writer was, returned home from the Staten Island Mall with a blue tie she'd bought off a Macy's sales rack and said, "You make us proud."

I had listened closely to Susan's advice about restraining emotion when talking about sensitive, controversial topics, about how to manage a room of funders. About how to make them feel like your own idea was theirs. Above all, look efficient. Look calm. Look absolutely always certain. This I told myself I could do.

I had spent most of my life trying to look efficient and calm. In high school, when I was up for a scholarship, I wore a blazer to the interview when everybody else wore sneakers and jeans. Later, in college classrooms, when a boy suggested that Puerto Rico was a welfare island, did I express any anger? No. I'd sat there and calmly pointed out the many different ways in which the United States had bled the island. And I did this with both the precision and arrogance of a bullied geek who had found himself all of a sudden captain of the debate team. I had learned this type of restraint from my father, whose advice to me when he dropped me off for my first job many years ago was this: "Keep your head down. Stay out of gossip. Don't get too close to anyone, and always do a good job."

But now, three years later, I realized Susan was a woman with an overinflated judgement of her own importance. And all of her kind words or gestures, even when they were directed at her own loyal, scrambling, and insecure staff, were manipulative. At a fundraiser, I'd once heard her exclaim, "How I've missed you. You must come by the office soon!" to a woman she'd described as boring and unimaginative during a staff meeting.

When the two of them hugged, Susan closed her eyes and smiled meaningfully in the same way I'd seen her smile at me sometimes when I made a program recommendation or if I suggested a revision that she didn't agree with.

"Interesting," she'd say. Nothing more. Then she would stand up from the conference table and pat my back.

Now, I stared an extra beat at her face so she could understand that I had heard her question and had chosen not to reply. The cooler burped up neon bubbles of water.

"Luis?" she asked.

I stood there and blinked.

Then I walked out the door.

* * *

Outside of our building you could see the harbor's gray water and the orange and blue boats ferrying commuters back and forth from Manhattan to the Island. The sun was cold and white. I walked along Richmond Terrace to the deli.

About five minutes further down the block you reach the Jersey Street projects where I'd grown up, a little bit before my parents moved out and rented the downstairs apartment of a small pink town house in West Brighton. Then there is about a mile and a half of trees and abandoned buildings that stretch along the water before you hit the children's museum, where my parents would take me and my sister when we were kids. There we would climb on the back of the giant green statue of a praying mantis that stood on the museum's lawn. And though we tried to scale the giant insect, we always ended up sliding down its neck. There are pictures hanging in my parents' hallway of me and my little sister sitting on its back, smiling, while the praying mantis's blank green face looks away.

I wanted to smoke. I could feel the urge lifting inside of me like a wave. So I bought a pack of cigarettes at the deli and smoked one as I walked along the traffic back to the office, burning away whatever had been squirming inside of my chest.

A string of about a dozen buses circled out of the terminal, winding around its long white ramps. The S62 pulled into the little shelter on Richmond Avenue and Bay Street, which was packed with a crowd of high schoolers who had just gotten out of Curtis.

When I pushed through the crowd to wave at the bus, I accidentally bumped into this teenage girl's book bag and she turned around and said, "Watch where the fuck you going." Then pushed me right back as the doors swung open to the bus.

I stumbled up the steps.

"Fucking animals," the bus driver said, pointing to the kids.

I ignored him, put the MetroCard in, and walked down the aisle of the bus searching people's faces for any type of reaction to the news about Pantaleo, for somebody to shake their head or mumble angrily to themselves like I had at my desk.

But nothing.

Mostly everybody was quietly looking at their phones as the bus bumped along the street. Two women in the back gossiped in Spanish about a coworker who had taken too many days off. And in a sudden burst of English the older one spat: "Bitch, you're not sick. Stop playing."

If anybody on that bus were to have talked at that moment about Garner and Pantaleo, I would have joined.

But the Island was silent.

As the bus turned onto Victory from Bay Street I looked out toward Tompkinsville Park at the makeshift memorial of flowers and candles next to the beauty supply store where he'd been killed.

All of a sudden I did not want to go back to my apartment at all. I got off at the next stop and walked back down to Bay Street to a local bar where once somebody had hung a dummy of Bin Laden with a noose around his head. It reminded me of a billboard from the early millennium—right after 9/11—that had featured a massive picture of a beheaded Bin Laden. Every time I went to the mall as a teenager, I'd pass it, the red strands of Bin Laden's neck dripping blood on invisible ground that escaped the billboard.

At the bar, I thought about texting a friend to join me, but it was only three o'clock and everybody I knew was at work. Or they no longer lived on the Island. I had been one of the few people who had stayed and felt strangely proud about it, even though part of me hated the Island, really hated it. I kept on coming back after college. People don't understand it because they've never seen the way the sky turns orange as it sinks into the water on your way back home from the city. The murals that stretch across Bay Street into Stapleton. Or the Liberian women waking up in the morning to set up the market in Park Hill, smoothing bright cloths on their tables before they arrange their goods. From all the Sri Lankan restaurants in St. George to the taquerias in Port Richmond. The mothers canvassing the block after a recent shooting with their pink Mothers Against Senseless Killings sweatshirts. The children scurrying from one table to the next, cutting out pink and green *papel picados* and skeleton puppets for El Día de Los Muertos.

I sat at the empty bar and ordered a beer, for a while swiping through the news on my phone, then stood up and went outside to smoke again. The water stretched horizontally in front of me, a gray moving boundary between the Island and the city. I was at that moment in drinking when everything seemed to unfold inside of my brain. All the edges felt both weirdly soft and clear.

My phone buzzed in my coat pocket and when I looked down I noticed it was Susan. When she called a second time, I sent it to voicemail. A minute later she texted: *I'm wondering when you're going to come back to the office.*

This was a very bold text for Susan. Usually, she would have been a little bit more strategic and begun tentatively with something along the lines of, "Hi, Luis, is everything OK?"

Of course, the concern would be practiced and artificial, but it would also indicate that she felt the need to preserve the illusion that she cared. Which of course meant that I was no longer an allowable cost when it came to her calculations of who deserved consideration. I was outside of budget.

When I went back inside, this time the bartender was a guy I recognized from high school. But we were never friends so we pretended not to know each other, which was fine. He didn't seem like the type of person I could commiserate with about the Pantaleo verdict. Though he was dressed in what looked like the affected uniform of Thoughtful and Socially Aware Artist, a long brown beard and ear plugs, I remembered how once in high school he'd laughed the loudest when another guy spat at me and said, "Hey Luis, this is Staten Island, not Puerto Rico. You're on the wrong island, man." I ordered another drink, swallowed it quickly, and then walked down Bay Street in the cold to the ferry.

On the boat, I sat outside and watched the water.

I had grown up on this ferry, had fallen asleep on it many times as a teenager coming back home from school or work, sometimes missing when it docked on Staten Island and mistakenly taking it back to Manhattan. Later, in my twenties, during the recession, when I couldn't find a decent job, I ate warm butter rolls in the morning on my way to work at Best Buy in Union Square. Those times I used pennies and nickels to buy coffee, counting them one by one on the counter with the Indian lady at the register, who would just let me have the cup if I was short a cent or two.

I was there on the boat when a group of women gasped and pointed out at the water: "A whale!" "No!" "Yes." "No." "It is. Look." Then we saw its blue body emerge from the water and curve back down into the steel Hudson River, its tail curling behind it, as one of the ladies called out: "What you doing in Staten Island, little buddy?"

Once, on the boat, after finishing my coffee, I found a dead roach at the bottom of the cup, its legs buried in the sugar.

I don't know why exactly I went to the city. There was no plan. I just knew I didn't want to be on the Island. I'd seen friends posting videos of protests, and thought maybe to join one. So I took the R train to Union

Square and found a crowd marching in the middle of traffic. Hundreds, thousands of people who would have scoffed at ever stepping foot on the Island now were animatedly marching for Garner, their figures disappearing between the traffic's blinking red, yellow, and green lights.

It took hours of walking in the cold and the crowd was uncertain, sometimes breaking off into separate smaller protests. I chose to stay with the crowd walking toward the boat, hoping whoever was leading the march had decided to try to take the protest to the Island.

But when we got to the terminal, we found that the cops had formed a barrier to block protesters from boarding the boat. Above their heads, gigantic electric blue letters spelling out *Staten Island Ferry* curved on top of the building's awning.

I pushed my way through the line of people in front of me until I reached a cop who put his hand out. "Not today."

"What do you mean not today?" I asked. "I live on the Island."

One of the cops went, *Pssh*, then said, "Yeah, right, guy."

"What do you mean, yeah right?" My hands trembled.

"Easy there, buddy."

A few of them stepped forward now and pushed me backwards. But I reached into the dark space in front of me to regain balance and caught myself before I could fall on an orange cone that tipped over and rolled comically down the street.

They had started to laugh now.

And I said, "Whether you like it or not. I live on the Island and you can't block me from taking the boat." I pushed myself between them.

With that, the cop gave a nod and more of them came now and surrounded me until I could feel myself falling on the ground between their legs.

Another protester had taken out a camera to record the scuffle, and I knew that within a few days a video would surface on Instagram or YouTube or CNN so that someone could watch me squirming on the ground while wondering, as they sipped their coffee, "Did he deserve it?" right before they minimized the window and scrolled on, right before finally x'ing out of the clip.

I knew this for sure, just as I was certain that I would walk into Susan's office that week and quit.

But I didn't care anymore. While I was on the ground a cop pushed his hand down on my chest as I tried to pull myself up by one of their legs. And I could hear myself saying in a voice that I could not recognize, wild and unpracticed and unstrategic, pointing over the harbor toward the Island: "Fuck you, I live there. That is where I'm from."

Who Would Break the Dark First

If you looked at the place, there wasn't anything really outwardly scary about it. I mean, it wasn't the type of haunted house that you would see on TV, with broken windows and creaking steps. There were no black cats or webs dripping from the window frames. Nothing you'd find on *Are You Afraid of the Dark?* No, this was a brand-new, skinny, white, two-story town house they built on Staten Island in the nineties, just as people started writing letters to the editor in the *Advance* about the Island being overdeveloped and crowded. *And the traffic! God, the traffic,* they wrote. Though by "crowded," I realize now they probably meant black and brown folks, aka my family.

We'd arrived in Staten Island in the early nineties fresh off the Verrazano Bridge from Brooklyn: Puerto Rican and loud. There were four of us: Mom, me, my little crazy epileptic sister Chrissy, and Mikey, the youngest, who that year was obsessed with Jim Carrey and ran around the house shouting, "Somebody stop me," his mouth permanently stained with SunnyD. The town house we ended up moving into was cheaply constructed on a tall hill. And whoever built it made the whole thing crooked, so that for years the house seemed to lean left entirely in one section as it sunk further into the ground. The wooden floor slanted in the living room. And there were strange gaps between the molding and the carpet. By the time my family had moved out of the house many years later, a crack had formed from the windowsill straight down to the floor. And behind the house was an old unkempt cemetery with forgotten graves that dated back to the early 1800s.

From the bedroom that the three of us kids shared, we could see the names of the gravestones with our binoculars. Up until then we'd lived in an apartment building in East New York with windows that just looked into the windows of other people's apartments. Below, there was a small concrete yard with clotheslines suspended from one sill to the next. The laundry and bed sheets trembled in the wind.

But this new shiny town house, this was some serious *Baby-Sitters Club* shit you'd see on TV. This was the type of place you'd catch on *Family Matters* or *Full House*. Who cares if it was crooked? We reveled in its exotic suburbanness, the string of pools that dotted our neighbors' backyards, our new HVAC system that banged out heat through the vents at night, warming up the whole house at once.

At first, the cemetery didn't even bother us. We made stories up about its ghosts, and sometimes when we played outside in our little yard, we'd have to jump over the chain-link fence to retrieve a ball that somebody had thrown over the gate into the tombstones and weeds. Chrissy was the best at jumping the fence; even in fifth grade, she was muscular and strong. (For years, when we were little kids, women would mistake Chrissy for a boy in the ladies' room and send her out, crying. And I'd have to comfort her in the car: "That woman's just mad because she was about to take a doo-doo and didn't want you to smell it... Hey, don't cry. I'll give you the blue Jolly Rancher, OK?") When the ball would land in the graveyard, Chrissy'd hop over the fence in one swift movement, then throw the ball back into our yard. Standing on the deck, we'd drop our arms over the fence and help pull her over to our side, hurriedly, as if something invisible was about to snatch her away.

* * *

Forget about the cemetery; in 1996, this was my mother's dream home. Young, Puerto Rican, single, and newly middle class, my mother did not detect any irony when she said she wanted to decorate the house "colonial." She bought expensive lace curtains on Sears credit to dress the windows. She even finally paid off a chinero she'd put on layaway at Macy's. Still, Brooklyn had made her superstitious. And ours was the only town house with black iron bars installed on all the windows to ward off burglars and a fake *Beware of the Dog* sign glued on the front door.

I was in seventh grade and my dreams were entirely different from my mother's. When I dreamt at night, it was about being able to buy a fifteen-dollar sweater at Wet Seal or a gold necklace with my name on it spelled in a bubbly font: *Ariella*. It was about getting a part in the school play or a good grade in earth science or about Anthony Caruso, who sat next to me in language arts and who had a beauty mark on his pointer finger, terrible chapped lips, braces, and bad breath. Outside of school, he made fun of my big forehead and wondered aloud to the other seventh-grade boys if I was Mexican or black.

And in all my foolishness I still loved him.

* * *

Those first few weeks, things were cool in our new life in the suburbs. We played outside and made a snowman, which proved harder to do in real life than on TV. We tried unsuccessfully to make friends with the neighbors' kids, who we saw had a pool all covered up for the winter.

We imagined spending our summers there dunking each other under the water. Newly emboldened, we even tried to convince my mom to get us a real dog, not just a hypothetical one, to scare away intruders.

At first, we didn't think anything about the strange noises at night. The dead, they didn't scare us. "It's the living you got to be afraid of," my mother would say. She'd grown up most of her life in the Gowanus projects, and she had this joke she liked to tell on the phone to all her girlfriends about the cemetery, pointing outside the sliding porch doors into its quiet darkness: "Best neighbors I ever had!"

But then one day Chrissy went downstairs to transfer the wet laundry from the washer to the dryer. She was untangling one of the white button-down shirts of her uniform from her dark blue jumper when she felt something lift her curly hair and slowly breathe on her neck. Chrissy spun around and screamed. The wet uniform she'd been holding fell on the dusty basement floor. Frantically, she looked around her, but there was no one else in the room. Just the tall furnace banging out hot air and some boxes of summer clothes stacked one on top of the other, shoved into a dark corner.

But the thing was, sometimes we did this to ourselves, let our minds play tricks on us. So it was easy for Chrissy to rationalize this by deciding that she had spooked herself out. She picked the uniform up from the floor, whipped it free of any dust balls, then shoved it into the dryer. But when she bent back down to pull more clothes from the washer, something in its dark well stirred against her fingers. Something with hair or fur. And legs. Something with a mouth. A mouse? A bug?

Chrissy tried to pull her hand away from the washer, but then something in the basin grabbed her fingers and pulled. A smell like vomit came from the machine and the grip twisted her hand so hard that she thought it might crush her fingers.

Me and Mikey were watching *Power Rangers* upstairs when we heard the scream curling in the air from the basement. We ran to the door to see what had happened, but she was already halfway up the stairs, talking about how a face had popped out from the dark and screamed at her while she was putting in laundry.

"I was just taking out the uniforms, minding my own business, then this Chuck E. Cheese–looking demon slid right in front of my face." She held out her own aching hand. "He crushed it."

At first, we didn't believe Chrissy. The year before we moved to the Island, she began getting seizures, and sometimes saw things when she blacked out. At school she had gotten into trouble various times for exaggerating. And whenever she told a story, she would add fake details, sometimes making herself out to look like the hero when she had in fact thrown the first punch.

Still, that week, Chrissy's story stayed with us and bloomed in our imaginations at night. We pictured hands reaching for us from underneath the bed. We did laundry in pairs now, and we were becoming very aware of the people buried underneath our house. That's why none of us wanted to go to the basement to get Christmas decorations when my mother tried to send us down.

"It's your turn, Ariella," Chrissy said.

She shook her big face with an attitude, and all the wires the doctors had glued to her head in order to measure her seizures the day before shifted against one another like beaded braids.

I was already doing the dishes, so we started to argue. I said something like, "(a) Chrissy, everybody knows that you're lazy. And you're just pretending to have epilepsy. And (b), don't talk to me like that. You're only in fifth grade."

Me, I was in seventh.

Then Mikey, who was the baby and my mother's favorite, said, "All I know is I'm not going down there, OK?"

Both me and Chrissy turned to where he was sitting at the table doing his homework with his gym uniform still on, his St. Augustine sweatshirt. The area on the table where he was sitting was sticky with the blue quarter water he'd spilt, and some of the juice had turned his teeth purple.

"Nobody was talking to you," Chrissy said, clapping the back of one of her hands against the palm of the other. "And if we're going down there, you're going down there too, asshole."

"Your mouth," my mother shouted from the living room. "All three of you take your crusty culos downstairs and find us the tree. Or no Christmas at all this year. I mean it."

We took this threat very seriously. None of my mother's warnings were empty. Once, on our way for ice cream sandwiches after school, she turned the car into the Hibachi Grill parking lot and drove straight back home because we wouldn't stop arguing with each other in the backseat about whether the green Power Ranger deserved to turn white and lead the others. "It's not fair. He's the most boring one," Chrissy'd said, to which Mikey responded, "You're boring."

So, the three of us had to figure out who would lead the line downstairs to the basement, who would reach for the chain that dangled from the ceiling to turn the light on, who would break the dark first.

"What if one of the ghosts grabs your hand while you're reaching for the chain? What would you do?" Chrissy asked.

I stared at her, hard. I said, "I'm not scared. I'll go first."

"I'll go in the middle," shouted Mikey, who probably thought he'd be safe sandwiched between us.

"What if something creeps up behind you and grabs your face like this?" I clutched Chrissy's forehead and shook it. Then Mami walked into the kitchen and yelled at me for touching her head.

* * *

The hardest part was the first step. Opening the basement door. Stepping down into the uncertain dark, which I imagined swallowing the three of us like quicksand. But really it wasn't the dark that we were afraid of. We were most frightened of what we'd see when we turned the light on.

Mikey put his sticky, smelly hand on my shoulder and giggled. And his giggling made Chrissy giggle. And Chrissy's giggling made me chuckle nervously, so that all three of us were laughing in the dark. When I finally found the switch and pulled it, light spread all over the basement, so that its walls and clutter looked harmless. The washing machine and the dryer hummed and clicked in the corner. The basement smelled like earth. We watched a hamper full of clothes vibrate on top of the washer, and there was a pair of Mikey's *Power Rangers* underwear drooping from the top of the dirty laundry. Once we got downstairs, Chrissy broke the line, ran to the hamper, and picked the underwear up with a broom, singing "Mikey got caca in his undies" while practicing the Running Man. When she waved the underwear in our direction, a spider fell out and he began to cry.

"No, I don't," he said. "I do not," as the spider scrambled into the boxes.

"Yeah, you do. That spider was eating your poop. *Nasty*," Chrissy said.

Now Mikey cried out even louder, and Mom opened the door and screamed at us to leave him alone. "Come upstairs. Now."

Mikey turned toward her voice and ran up the steps. "Chrissy's making fun of me, again."

"Liar," Chrissy shouted, following him.

Alone in the basement, I took one last look at the walls around me. What was there to be afraid of? Unpainted drywall? A concrete floor? I looked at the plastic tree folded in upon itself, lying in the corner, covered in dust. Green strands of dead Christmas lights snaked around its flattened branches.

* * *

Mom stepped on one arm of the couch with her bare foot so that I could see the pretty pale bump of her very skinny ankle. "Cogalo. Quick. Come on, guys," she said, then had each one of us grab a side of the tree as she tried to screw on the top.

But the fake pine needles kept on scratching Mikey. And Chrissy got upset because she realized that he had stopped holding his side of the branches and was just pretending.

In my mother's hands, the top of the tree kept on popping off. "Damnit, esa mierda."

We stood there like that, all four of us battling with the branches, until my mother finally got it to stand up.

And when it was time to put up the lights, Mikey asked Ma if he could plug Chrissy's head into the tree, laughing like he was on an episode of *Pinky and the Brain*, the morning's sleep still attached to the corner of his crusty eyelids.

"That's why nobody likes you," Chrissy said. "Go wipe your face."

Until Mom told the both of them to stop it. "Each of you, come," she said holding a gray strand of plastic pearls between her long, red nails.

Then we each grabbed a piece and helped her wrap the garland around the tree.

* * *

In 1996, I was obsessed with science, how the cell could open and shut like an eye. At my new school, Mrs. Caputo, my social studies teacher, had put in a recommendation for me at the Guilford Special High School of Math and Science. For the application, I was writing an essay about all of my twelve-year-old girl goals. I was going to become a scientist or an engineer. A molecular biologist! A surgeon . . . I was going to have five kids. All of this while dancing backup for Mariah Carey.

At night, Ma tucked Chrissy in to make sure the wires on her head were still attached to this machine that measured what her brain looked like asleep.

Chrissy agreed to let me look at it. "Just don't press anything, OK?"

I tugged at each wire gently so that it wouldn't fall off her head.

"Dr. Malinga says it's my neurons. They're being wacky."

And from my side of the room, I could see Mikey sit up in his bed, the silhouette of his curly fro. "I'm telling mom that you're cursing again."

Chrissy whipped her head up from the bed. "I said neuron, not moron." She threw a pillow at him. "You moron."

* * *

Our house was identical to the six other houses on the block: pink vinyl siding, a gray roof, and a small bay window where you could see the Christmas tree we put up. All of the houses on this street looked like imitations of real homes—something a little boy slammed together with LEGOs and blocks. Each one had a wooden patio that overlooked the front yard in which a skinny tree grew from a small circle of black store-bought soil.

This was Mami's dream house, and in twenty years of mortgage payments she planned to own it. *Look*, she said, pointing to a picture in the newspaper the first day she saw a photo of the house. *That's where we're moving next. And doesn't that look perfect?* Much better than a two-bedroom apartment in Brooklyn, where you can't even play outside during the winter because somebody's already let their dog piss all over the snow.

But in real life the house looked different than the picture in the newspaper. If you walked behind the cluster of homes and looked past the chain-link fence that surrounded the yards, you could see the beginning of the cemetery. And three blocks away there was a men's halfway house where sometimes the men sitting outside would try to talk to Ma.

There were some problems with the house, too. The cabinets wouldn't shut right, so sometimes they hung open, no matter how many times Mom screwed in the clasps. Then the bedroom doors would get stuck shut, and it would take both my and Chrissy's combined muscle to yank them open. Sometimes the garbage disposal got backed up and the food would somehow travel to the bathroom sink, where it would rise, gray and murky, and spill on the counter.

Also, our neighbors were assholes. When Mami came through with three brown, loud-ass kids and no husband, they threw some serious adult shade at her that even I noticed as a twelve-year-old kid. Sometimes they knocked on the door and complained that we were making too much noise while we played *Mario Kart* or that the TV was too loud on Friday nights when Ma bought us pizza and let us stay up late to watch TGIF.

When Mami went all out and bought a five-foot blow-up Santa to decorate the lawn for Christmas and celebrate our first year in a real house, one of the neighbors left a passive-aggressive note taped on our door complaining that our Christmas decorations were tacky and loud. No signature. "Because they already know," my mother said. "Pendejos." She ripped up the letter outside, hoping whoever wrote it saw her shred it to pieces. Then inside the house she went on a tirade to an invisible audience: "Fuck do I care what you think about my Christmas decorations.

Like you pay my bills. I'm paying for this house with my own hard-earned money, just like you are."

Next day, she woke up early, went to Caldor's, and returned home with a three-foot plastic reindeer she'd gotten 15 percent off on sale. We watched her from the window as she stuck our discounted Rudolph right next to the blow-up Santa, snow falling on her slick black curly hair. The reindeer's lit-up nose blinked red every night that winter. And Mami left it there even after Christmas, until we got hit with that big snow storm in 1997. We dug poor Rudolph out from under twenty inches of snow, finally, on January 9th.

* * *

Fifth period, during social studies, Mrs. Caputo stood in front of the board fumbling with the projector.

"Not a lot of people realize it, but Staten Island was the original Ellis Island," she said, lifting one finger in the air.

In the 1800s there was a hospital in Tompkinsville where they quarantined waves of German and Irish immigrants, who were suspected of being sick: cholera, yellow fever, smallpox. People on the Island hated the hospital. They thought that the immigrants were dirty. Once, a yellow fever epidemic broke out on the Island, killing thirty people. And when the state tried to move the hospital to the South Shore, the Island residents, fed up, went to the unfinished building one night and torched it. Which now, thinking about it (after ten years of living here), is such a Staten Island thing to do: "Not in my backyard!" As if they had forever owned the land which was never theirs to begin with. They'd pushed out the Native Americans who lived on the Island without even ever really knowing their name.

After she got the projector to work, Mrs. Caputo showed us these old newspaper illustrations drawn in black ink of the fire consuming the hospital, the little illustrated men celebrating and dancing around the smoke like a coven of witches. In the drawing the artist left the empty space of the flames white.

After school that day I took out my social studies textbook and pointed out the different pictures of immigrants to Mikey and Chrissy while reading the captions aloud. On one page there was a line of women wearing black waiting to be processed, on another an Italian family who they wouldn't let in because the mother had started to cough.

"I would never let them take my mom," Chrissy said.

Mikey dragged a finger against the picture. "How come all those olden-time people never smile?" Then he pointed to the gray head of one of the immigrants. "Even that old baby looks mean," he said, squinting and pushing out his lips to imitate the infant's expression. "You *mean* old baby."

"Stupid." Chrissy pulled the textbook away from him. "He's sick."

* * *

One day, Chrissy had the bright idea to reach out to the ghosts. She thought that perhaps we could make peace with them if only we could all just sit down and talk. I suspected it had something to do with the fact that St. Augustine had added a conflict resolution section to the fifth-grade curriculum, and I was skeptical. In all of the horror movies I'd ever seen there were always a couple of dumb kids who dragged out a Ouija board, contacted some three-hundred-year-old evil-ass spirit they had no business talking to, and then proceeded to die in violent and horrific ways. Me, I wanted to survive. I wanted to live just long enough to get accepted into the Guilford Special High School of Math and Science.

Chrissy's plan also had some problems. For example: how does one even talk to a ghost? On this point we argued for several hours. My mother would never let a Ouija board into the house. She was very superstitious and had grown up various versions of Christian as a child in the types of churches that later would proclaim that the Harry Potter books were evil.

So Chrissy had to improvise. She reached up and turned off the lights and Mikey flicked on a flashlight. I wanted no part of it at all and threatened to get Mom, until Chrissy warned me she wouldn't tell me about her epilepsy anymore if I didn't participate.

"Fine. But I'm telling you right now it's not going to work."

With that I sat down on the bed with her and Mikey, and we all held hands.

With the wires hanging from her head and her eyes shut, Chrissy looked like some type of strange psychic. "Hello, dear ghosts," she said, then shifted a little bit and straightened up her back. "We are your new neighbors, Christina, Ariella, and Michael Delgado, and we are calling you to make peace." She was talking like a preacher now, elongating the words, deepening her voice. "If you hear us, please give us a sign."

When I laughed, she opened her eyes and said "Don't ruin this" in such a serious tone that I closed my mouth. "Are you there, you poor, troubled spirit?"

The three of us stood there holding hands like that for about thirty seconds before Mikey announced, "I need to pee."

"Michael!" Chrissy threw her hands in the air. "Not yet."

All of our eyes were open now and the room was dark except for a small circle of light that the flashlight cast against the wall. There we saw our three shadows as we sat cross-legged on the bed, clutching each other's hands. The border of blue and red animal faces—bears, zebras, lions—that Ma had pasted along the top of the wall seemed to grimace at us.

"OK, I don't think this is going to work."

But Chrissy stopped me with one hand and pointed at the wall.

"Look," she said.

I couldn't believe it. Another shadow now stepped behind the three of us into the circle of light. It stood above our crouching figures, then raised a hand and waved at us.

All three of us screamed.

Mikey popped up from the circle and pointed at Chrissy. "You did that."

"No, I didn't."

"Yeah, you did that with your hands."

"How, stupid?" Chrissy popped up from the bed now and pushed him. And the two of them ran down the stairs arguing. I picked up the flashlight from the bed and tried to replicate the shadow with my own fingers. But I couldn't do it, no matter how much I played with the light.

* * *

Chrissy's doctor was only about ten blocks away from us, situated in a little strip mall next to a supermarket with pink stucco walls. Stranded, rusty shopping carts moved by themselves in the breeze across the parking lot. We went there once a week to check what was happening inside of Chrissy's head.

One day Mami drove up to the house after work around six o'clock and honked the horn so that we could take Chrissy to an appointment. We were upstairs getting ready, and Mikey was making a lot of noise turning his boxes of toys upside down, trying to find his other sneaker. Chrissy was quickly finishing up a bowl of cereal, slurping the milk down. And I was in the kitchen looking for my copy of the house keys to lock the door.

Mikey came in with his lost shoe dangling from his fingers by the laces.

"Hurry up. Mami's waiting." I pointed to the door.

Mikey tied his shoes and ran down the stairs to the car, his book bag slapping behind him with each step. And from the upstairs window, I could see him sliding open the door to our old yellow van. Mom grabbed his face to kiss it. Then Chrissy slowly walked over to join them in her St. Augustine gym uniform sweats with the brain wave machine clipped to her waist. It was gonna be a bad day for Chrissy; Mom already knew it. So she let her sit in the front seat. I watched them huddled in the car, the smoke curling away from the exhaust pipe in the cold. It began to flurry now around them so that they looked as if they were trapped inside a snow globe.

I went back to the kitchen and kept on searching for the house keys, but

I couldn't find them. Not on top of the counter or in the junk drawer, not in my pockets or in my book bag. The appointment was in five minutes, and it was a ten-minute drive. Mami impatiently honked the horn. Next, I looked in the apple-shaped cookie jar we kept on the kitchen table, but there was nothing there.

From inside the house I could hear my mother honk the horn again. I ran to the living room and slid open the window. "Ma, I can't find the keys."

My mother stepped out of the car. "What?"

"The keys, I can't find them."

Snow had gathered on top of her black hair. She shook her head and made her way into the house. Once inside, all of her jewelry echoed as she ran up the stairs and into the kitchen. "Did you check the cookie jar?" Angry.

"Of course," I said, maybe too loudly, to which she raised one pointer finger and answered, "Your mouth, watch it."

Then she reached into the jar anyway, because she never trusted me. By that time I was pushing thirteen. And I was no longer cute like Mikey or Chrissy. I was half child and half adult. And my mother interpreted everything I said as a threat. If I wanted macaroni and cheese instead of spaghetti, if I decided to buy the red shirt instead of the pink one, or if I took longer in the bathroom than usual: "So, now, you think you're grown?"

I heard the keys before I saw them angrily chattering in Ma's hand. She'd pulled them out of the same cookie jar that only two minutes ago was empty.

And I stood there.

In disbelief.

"You know, Ariella," she said, then just shook her head and went down the stairs.

And there's no science that can explain that.

* * *

"So it looks like we're seeing some seizure activity," said Dr. Malinga.

We liked him. At home, we often imitated Dr. Malinga doing the hokey pokey. When he said the word "seizure," he chuckled as if the brain wave machine were telling him a joke. Like, no big deal—just a little epilepsy, young lady.

C-sure Activity, I wrote in my notebook.

"Would you mind terribly," he asked, "if we keep it on for another few days?"

Chrissy nodded but then crossed her arms and stared at the corner of the doctor's office, where a gigantic chart of the brain hung, its cerebral hemisphere highlighted in dark green.

Already, at school, the other students had started calling her Frankenstein and chucking pieces of steamed cafeteria carrots at her uniform. Already, Jimmy, who lived next door to us, had asked Chrissy in homeroom if she had cancer.

Ma patted Chrissy's head. "Only a few more days, baby."

At night, in my application, I wrote: *Epilepsy is a terrible disorder that my sister has.* I wrote about the wires and the machine. *If accepted into the Guilford Special School of Math and Science, I would like to find a cure.* I cringe thinking about it now, how eager I was to get into that school, how I would have told them anything to be accepted, even if it meant describing my own sister's pain.

* * *

Who knows how it started? Or even where it began? The doctor could not explain. This is what Ma told Titi Jessy on the phone: "It could be anything." There was, after all, that time Chrissy fell while she was climbing on the counter when she was four. Possibly she hit her head too hard on the floor. The body can be funny and unforgiving. Shit, my mother said, things had happened to both her and Titi when they were kids that still hurt them.

I had my own questions. "What does it feel like?" I asked. "The seizures?"

Chrissy and I were sitting in the kitchen watching the snow. Mikey was asleep.

"Like nothing," she said.

"Nothing?"

"Most of the time, you don't even remember it."

She was eating a cookie. And in the kitchen we could hear Mami snore. Frequently, now, we went downstairs in the middle of the night to eat when we couldn't sleep without the sounds of traffic or a passing train. In the quiet, you started to hear other things more clearly: the rustle of branches outside, the way that a house shifts and moves as it settles further into the ground.

"You were like this," I said, "the last time it happened."

I threw myself on the floor and swung my arms.

Chrissy grinned with the cookie in her mouth. "You're stupid." Then scratched one of her wires. "It tastes funny."

"What?"

"Before it happens, it has a funny taste."

Later that night I dreamt that I woke up to go to the bathroom because something was swimming inside of me, moving back and forth like a fish. When I looked in the mirror, my face was yellow. The insides of my eyes were red. And blood fell out when I opened my mouth to scream.

It was Chrissy who shook me until I woke up because she saw me fidgeting and trembling in the bed. When I began to tell her the dream, she interrupted and said, "And you threw up blood?"

"How did you know?" I asked her.

"Because in my dreams, the same thing happens to me."

* * *

At school the next day, the teachers let Chrissy wear a hat, which partially covered her wires, but not all of them. You could still see some of the cords hanging down her back.

Worse, they were multicolored.

For the first half of the day, things went well. Most of the kids had gotten used to seeing Chrissy walking down the hall with this strange machine attached to her head. Sometimes when I saw her in the hallways as we changed classes I pulled on one of the wires, and she turned around as if she was going to fight me, but then she grinned. Some of the boys called her a robot, but Chrissy'd always been good about a comeback. "That's why your mouth smells like fart," she'd tell them.

Some of the other sixth-grade girls felt sorry for her. They thought, *Poor Chrissy, she's dying.* They said, "You know, those wires actually look kind of pretty!" And then they'd stroke one of the dangling pieces of plastic with their hand.

In my science class, I handed in my personal statement to Mrs. Caputo, who said she would be sending the application via Priority Mail.

"What a very touching essay about your sister," she said. And that in two weeks we would know if I got in.

* * *

I spent those two weeks praying and making deals with god. In my negotiations, I told him that if I got into the Guilford School, I would pray four times a day. I would pay attention during church. I would help Ma out more around the house.

"Ariella," Mikey said from across the room. "Can you please, please, please shut up?"

From my bed I could hear Chrissy pray out loud, too. Though her prayers were different.

Dr. Malinga made her keep the wires on a third week, and within that time the girls in her class had lost interest and sympathy. Now, Chrissy's sickness bored them.

And now there were too many boys to fight back when they teased Chrissy, even if she had a smart comeback. There were more boys than her. And if they made fun of her all at once, even if she yelled, it did not matter because their voices would drown hers. And no one would be able to hear how smart her comeback was.

* * *

On the third day of the second week of waiting, Mrs. Caputo stopped me after earth science. She said, "Ariella, dear, come sit down." Then passed me a letter from the Guilford Special School of Math and Science that read, *We regret to inform you that you have not been selected for the class of 1997.*

"This has nothing to do with you," Mrs. Caputo said. "You are a talented lady and very qualified."

I liked Mrs. Caputo's voice and her short curly brown hair and the way she talked about earthquakes, but this explanation did not help.

On the bus ride home that day, I listened to the kids scream and laugh and throw paper balls out the window. I listened to them experiment with insulting each other. So I didn't even notice that Chrissy was not on the bus until Jimmy from next door slid next to me and explained how Mr. De la Rosa was at the board writing out an equation when all of a sudden the whole class heard something rattle and then crash. Chrissy had started shaking, and her pencil case fell and slid across the floor.

Everybody turned around to watch her bang against the desk.

And beneath her seat there was a dark pool of piss.

* * *

That day Chrissy came home an hour late. "Don't talk to me," she said. "Nobody talk to me." Then she went upstairs.

"What's up with *her*?" Mikey asked while trying keep his Mario Kart from falling off Rainbow Road.

I slapped the back of his head.

"What?" he said, fake innocently, as he rubbed it.

When Ma called on the phone, she asked, "Where's Chrissy? Is she okay?" They wouldn't let Ma leave work so that she could pick Chrissy up at school that day, so she was worried. "Ariella, please make sure she's all right. I won't be home till at least seven o'clock."

I heated up yesterday's rice and chicken and, when it was done, called everybody to the table to eat. But when Chrissy came down, we all gasped.

Mikey said, "Ooooh, Ma's going to be mad. You ripped all the wires out of your head."

Chrissy was standing there, her face red, pieces of glue still stuck to her hair where the wires formerly had been attached. She started to cry.

"Shut up," I told Mikey, and stood up to hug her.

"Soon enough," he shouted, "the both of you are going to learn to respect me."

Which made Chrissy laugh. Then we all sat down to eat. The rice which had tasted so good last night was small and hard today. The lights on the Christmas tree took turns blinking red, then green, then blue. It was only six thirty, but outside it was completely dark. Mikey, he burped softly, put his plate in the sink, then went to the living room to turn on the TV.

And that's when we heard a boom from downstairs, as if a shelf had collapsed in the basement, breaking a dozen different boxes. The three of us froze. "Whoa," said Mikey. "What was that?"

Downstairs we heard a footstep creak against the wood. Then two.

"Ma?" I called out.

"Shush," said Chrissy. "That's not Mom, and you know it."

She picked up a knife. The two of us followed her to the basement door, which she opened. In this new dark, we heard another footstep. Was it mine? Was it yours? Someone shut the door behind us. And now it was completely black. Mikey screeched and rocked back and forth as he tried to catch his breath between sobs. I turned around and tried to open the door but it was stuck.

"Whatever you are," Chrissy said, "we're not scared of you. And you better leave us alone. This is our home, too."

Then she reached for the light.

As Luck Would Have It

Imagine thousands of millions of lights twitching along the various ceilings of New York's five boroughs—office buildings, brownstones, town houses, projects, and bodegas—then, poof: dying all at once. The hot trains stuck underneath the city, and all of the people crawling out of their doors, then along the wet, dark tunnels, unable to see. Arms extended in front of them like antennae as the roaches scurry away from their fingers.

My cousin's wife tells me that after the second hour stuck underground, a businesswoman on the N train started rocking in her seat, then suddenly broke out into this monologue about terrorist attacks, until a sixteen-year-old summer counselor in a JCC camp T-shirt told the woman to sit down and shut the fuck up: "You're scaring my kindergarteners! See!" In the scant light of their cell phones, one of the five-year-olds started to weep behind his X-Men book bag.

This was the blackout of 2003.

By midnight, the Long Island and New Jersey folks trying to get home gave up and lay down on the long steps of Penn Station. They unfolded their morning newspapers and draped them across the concrete like bedsheets. The rest of the folks, who were lucky enough to be at home when the lights went out, tried to figure out how to wipe their asses in the dark and whether or not going to the bathroom really warranted the use of a candle. Later, while they slept, the food rotted inside of their warm refrigerators.

Some folks became Good Samaritans and decided to direct traffic, and some folks decided to break shit or sell eight-dollar bottles of water. I tell you, take light and air conditioning and public transportation away from a people, and watch them become who they really are.

Me?

I had to walk two hours from my job at the DMV on 31st Street to the Staten Island Ferry, which was no small task. Ever since the baby, even though it had already been a year, it was like my body was telling me to go fuck myself. True, I had little Danny, and I loved picking him up and feeding him and watching his face expand. But now, I also had hemorrhoids. In the shower, my hair came out in handfuls. And peeing was never the same again. If I laughed too happily or sneezed, that was it.

It took me six months to recover from the c-section, and every dark part of me stung. The first two weeks, my mother had to help me walk to the bathroom to pee. Moral of the story: you don't just magically recover from trying to deliver vaginally for ten hours and then having your belly cut open and your organs rearranged instead.

By the time I got to the terminal, I was drenched in sweat. The sun was making me nauseous. A thick crowd surrounded the building, and some construction workers in front of me started talking about how the ferry service had been suspended. Indefinitely.

"Does anybody know what's going on?" I tried to ask, but my voice got swallowed in the commotion.

And I had to sidestep a ten-year-old who was out there hustling in front of the closed-down 1 train, trying to sell me a fifteen-dollar flashlight. "You sure? I got batteries, too, miss," he said, pointing to a Century 21 bag full of AAs.

"No, thank you," I said, then on second thought, turned around. "All right, give me a couple of packs."

After spending twenty dollars on batteries, I tried to inch my way closer to the terminal through the crowd.

A man sweating through his blue dress shirt paced back and forth in front of the terminal repeating one word over and over again into his Blackberry: "Unfuckingbelievable."

* * *

An hour passed.

And then one more.

My mother, who was taking care of the baby at home, was more apocalyptic over the phone than ever. "Do you have your Mace? Food? Water?"

"Yes, Ma," I said, then told her about the batteries.

"Listen, I just got off the phone with your Aunt Linda. And I want you to call your cousin Tommy and tell him to pick you up at the terminal. And also, we need eggs. And bread. And toilet paper, too. And cold cuts. Low sodium. Not the cheap stuff either, Julie. If he starts to argue about it, tell him he still owes me twenty dollars."

Why she was asking for eggs and cold cuts when the electricity was down, I have no idea.

"That's not really possible, Ma. The traffic's not even moving." And I wasn't lying either. I had outwalked all of the cars in Midtown that were stuck on Broadway. "And what do you need toilet paper for? We have a whole closet full," I said, which she ignored.

"You know what, sweetheart? You can walk across the Williamsburg Bridge and maybe Tommy can pick you up from there."

The Williamsburg Bridge! I looked down at my broken Mary Janes. A blister the size of a grape was bubbling up on the back of my right ankle. "There's no way I'm walking to Brooklyn right now, Mom."

"So what are you going to do, Julie?" she shouted, loud enough that the person next to me heard it and chuckled.

"Why are you screaming at me? I'm not the one who did this. I'm not ConEd. I don't control the electricity."

"Julie, what are you going to do?"

"I don't know. Maybe I'll find a seat at the terminal and fall asleep here," I said, but when I looked around, all of the benches were taken, and there were people sitting on top of their book bags and briefcases on the floor.

My mother, she almost had an aneurysm. "The terminal!"

I had to move the phone away from my ear because that's how loud she was.

"No, I don't like it," she said. "I don't like it at all, you sleeping on the ground with a bunch of creeps."

"OK, Ma, look, I gotta go."

"Do you have money?"

"Ma, I have to go."

"I said, 'Do you have any money?'" she asked louder.

"Yes. Don't worry."

Though the truth was I only had a five-dollar bill left, and all the ATMs didn't work, so I couldn't take out any cash.

The baby started to cry on my mother's side, which distracted her. "OK, look, sweetheart. Just get home?"

After we hung up, I found a spot of floor next to the ATM and sat down and waited.

I never considered myself a lucky person. So I was surprised when they finally started letting people on the boat, and I was in the first group.

On the ferry, the sun fell, and everything became dark. It was the first time I'd ever seen the New York Harbor without an arc of lit-up skyscrapers.

* * *

This was the year I had recently started praying again. I had stopped before because of other stuff that is too long and boring to get into right now. But, basically, all you need to know is that I stopped, even in spite of my many years of Catholic school that my poor single mother worked so hard to pay for, until I figured out the trick to talking to god. You can't ask for specific things—because in the end you don't know what's going to be good for you. It's like an Aesop fable: somebody makes a wish to be rich, they win the lottery or find a buried treasure, and then end up getting murdered in their sleep by their father for their money.

I never really prayed to be rich. But I did spend most of my twenties trying to ask for very specific things, and it was like I was texting god and he wasn't returning my phone calls. On my way home after work on the bus I'd catch myself saying things like, "In the name of the Father, the Son, and the Holy Spirit, please get Michael to leave his wife, already. And be a real father to Danny." I'd say, "Our Father, who art in Heaven, make Michael a better person. Get Michael to actually love me." And god would take a while to respond. He'd see me sending out the Bat-Signal, and then like three weeks later I'd accidentally tip over a cup of coffee on the kitchen table, or an overdraft fee would land in my account. And I knew that was just god's way of being like: Fuck Michael. So I'd tell god, I'd say: "All right, fair enough. I deserve that. I mean, it *is* adultery, BUT: can I at least get a job that pays me more than thirteen dollars an hour?"

And god didn't like that, because I suppose he thought I was being cute. But for me, it was more like: I'm Just Being Real, Man. Give me a nice boss. Give me an hour for lunch. Give me SOMETHING.

And it was like god was telling me, "Stop saying 'Give Me,' Julie."

But this is how I learned how to pray: That night when I finally got back to the Island, I was digging through my purse for my keys with Danny squiggling in the car seat on the stoop. I was smacking the mosquitos away from his face with the other hand. My heart started to beat faster because I couldn't feel the keys. I couldn't find them and my mom was at a doctor's appointment so no one was home.

I ended up having to yank the kitchen window open and crawl over the sill, careful as I balanced myself over that window so that I wouldn't land on the sharp raised molding of the window frame. The smell of burnt coffee hit me because I had forgotten to turn the pot off and the dishes were mounded in the sink. From inside the kitchen, I could hear the baby starting to cry.

When I scrambled back to the door, Danny was not happy. He looked up at me as if I had betrayed him, as if I had abandoned him for years on that stoop instead of just minutes to unlock the door. I knelt down to unbuckle him from the baby chair and whispered, "Stop crying, baby, my love." Then Danny started flailing his arms when I stood up and popped me right in the fucking face. I could taste the cut on the inside of my lip opening, a sliver of blood that tasted like silver. And I couldn't take it anymore. I put Danny down, squeezed my hands against my mouth, and said: "God, just make me happy. Whatever the fuck you want. Whatever you think will make me happy, all right?" Then it was as if he drew the clouds away to peek down at me.

Suddenly, the baby stopped. The blood inside my lip evaporated or rather retreated into the skin, rewinding itself. The apartment became still, and I felt as if I could breathe more clearly now; all of a sudden, it was as if the way I had been breathing before was not breathing at all.

* * *

In 2003, I had this joke. When people asked me what I did for a living, I liked to tell them I took pictures. Folks always thought that was a big thing, like I might be some type of photographer, until they realized I just worked for the DMV, where I snapped headshots of the tired and angry masses of New York City for their photo IDs.

I remember there was this one woman. When it was her turn, she started flinging her utility bills at me through the window

"Your Social," I said, sorting through the paperwork.

"What?"

"I need your Social."

She shook her head, the white gold infinity pendant rising and falling against her reddening freckled chest. Then she flitted through her purse until she found her Social Security card, which disappointed me.

I would have liked nothing more than to send that woman away without an ID because she was missing a required form of identification. The light on the ceiling vibrated and then dimmed.

I looked at the card, marked the paperwork, and then flicked the Social through the window back at her so that it slid a good distance across the counter and fell on the floor.

"Jesus," she said, for a second disappearing from the window as she bent down to find the card. After a minute or two, finally she stood up.

"Look at the camera, please," I said.

"Where's the camera?"

I pointed at the very obvious camera hanging from the corner of the booth.

"I don't see it."

I pointed again. "The camera."

"Oh, that."

Then the woman straightened her shoulders and practiced various versions of duck face, each one sucking more of her cheeks underneath her cheek bones. Duck face to the left. Duck face to the right. Duck face, chin pointed down, peering straight into the camera.

This was the only part of the job I liked: watching people adjust their faces for a picture. Looking at their slight agitated movements on the screen, the way their faces twitched as they worked so hard to appear as what they wanted everybody else to see.

"You need to look straight into the camera, miss."

I snapped a shot and caught this benevolent version of Christina Harris. Pink lipstick. Dark eyebrows. Tilting her head ever so slightly to the right so that the camera would catch her left cheekbone, the glimmering diamond in her ear.

But I sighed in pretend frustration. Made a big deal of shaking my head. "Oh, dear. It didn't work," I said. "Too dark. Let's try again."

"Really?" Christina Harris groaned, and the pink smile evaporated from her face as she rolled her eyes.

"Really. Let's try again."

I held my index finger above the mouse and watched the cursor waver above the little icon of the camera.

Immediately, she smiled again—the grimace gone. Even though I had tried to snap the picture quickly to capture the frown, she had somehow been able to pose and transform into sweet, kind Christina in less than half a second. In this new shot she looked as if she were playfully beckoning for whoever looked at her picture to laugh at a joke.

"Ugh," I said. "Can you keep your head still?"

"What?"

"You moved too quick, and now the picture's blurred."

"Are you fucking kidding me?" she said.

Then she pinched her lips in frustration, which was when I finally caught the shot of her face that I wanted. Lopsided and unsymmetrical.

But I pretended that I hadn't taken the picture yet.

"OK, one, two, three, now smile," I said.

Again, kind, playful Christina radiated from the frame, an eyebrow aggressively raised, her mouth wide open as she smiled, but of course I had beat her to it and already taken the picture to capture who she really was. "Got it!"

"Is it good?" she said.

"Very good."

"Could I see it?"

"Sure." I grinned and turned the computer around so she could glimpse the screen which caught her face pinched in anger.

"Oh." She grimaced at the photo. Horrified.

And there was nothing as satisfying as watching her realize how ugly she looked in all of her condescending anger.

"You'll get your ID in the mail in three weeks," I told her. "Please step aside."

Then I apologized to god for my pettiness and pressed a button for the next person to come up.

* * *

Weekdays that whole year, I woke up at six in the morning, crept quietly past my mother's room to make sure she was OK, and put the coffee on while I showered. Afterwards, in a towel, I'd bump into my bedroom in the dark to search for a pair of stockings that still fit me. By that time, the baby would be crying, reaching his hands toward the blue night-light glowing above his bed. And I'd feed him while my mother poured herself a cup of coffee.

Before I left, she would take Danny from my arms and whisper in his ear, "Who's the handsomest baby in the world? Who is he?"

Danny would return her question with wet laughter, his fat arms reaching for her face.

"You are! You are, my love."

* * *

There's a quiet section of the boat where people are supposed to not talk or make loud noises. Mornings I would sit there and close my eyes sometimes to try to get another twenty minutes of mediocre sleep while the boat moved across the water. One terrible morning I needed this sleep so badly, I used my purse as a pillow and leaned my head against a column. The buckle was pinching my cheek, so I took my scarf off and wrapped it around my purse.

My mother had been up that night sick, the worst she'd been in a while, and I couldn't bear to leave her like that alone all night, sitting on the couch wincing in front of the TV. We drank coffee and watched old *Law & Order* episodes until three thirty in the morning, when we fell asleep together on the couch. Two hours later, I woke up.

On the boat, just as I wavered off to sleep, I heard a thump. Somebody had dropped a heavy bag of what sounded like metal on the floor next to me. I'm not opposed to people noisily sitting down. It's a free country. But then, just as I was about to fall back to sleep, I opened my mouth, breathed in, and swallowed what smelled like a combination of scrambled egg and sauerkraut.

And here is where I object: farting at six thirty in the morning next to a defenseless sleeping person—now, that is unforgivable. I opened my eyes to look at the perpetrator, who was beginning a very loud conversation on his phone in the Quiet section, mind you. He looked familiar but I couldn't quite place him right away until he shouted, "These people are unfuckingbelievable."

It was the man who had been pacing back and forth in front of the terminal the day of the blackout. Now he waved an agitated fist to punctuate each syllable as if he were knocking on a door with his curled up index finger. "Just tell her we'll put up more money for the street fair." When he bit into his bacon, egg, and cheese, the yolk spilled down his lip and dripped onto his blue tie.

"Shit." He took a napkin out and tried to wipe the yolk away with a downward motion that only pushed the yellow goo further into the fabric. "Just buy them a fucking bouncy house or something. Jesus, it's not that difficult. Do we really have to spend this time arguing over an elementary school Halloween party?"

He was shaking his head now.

"You know what? I don't care about Mrs. Ellen. If Mrs. Ellen has something to say to me, tell her to come to the office and say it to my face. She thinks just because she rules that fifth grade, she can talk to whoever, however she wants to talk. Well, you know what, I'm not eleven years old. And not for nothing, you think that school would be a little bit more grateful that Richard, Ross, and Russo is donating to their Halloween events."

It went on like that for another ten minutes until he lost connection in the middle of the water. "Sarita?"

Nothing.

"Are you there? Sarita? Goddamnit."

He sighed, pulled the phone away from his face, and looked around self-consciously. Then closed his eyes and began to snore so loudly that I just stood up, gathered my things, and made my way to the front of the boat.

* * *

The DMV is like purgatory, and there's no telling how long it will take before they let you out for your sins. We liked to call Barbara the gatekeeper. She was this child-sized Puerto Rican woman who herded folks into different lines.

We all laughed when once a confused teenage boy trying to take his permit test came up to her and asked, "Do you work here?"

She looked at him and frowned: "Unfortunately."

The next minute a construction worker, who'd been pushing his bag of tools with his foot, put his hands up and said "Motherfucker" upon realizing he had been waiting on the wrong line for half an hour. His orange cap swung from his belt in anguish.

"You mean I have to come back?" another woman said to the teller at a window, her two-year-old pouring orange juice on her foot. "I can't get another day off of work."

On the radio, Bette Midler sang "God is watching us" the whole time.

Later, a skinny woman came up to my kiosk. She had short, thin, silvery-brown hair that looked like it was growing in, while some pieces were broken. When she came up to the counter, she placed a folder through the slot and smiled politely, saying, "Good morning. How are you today?"

She was missing one form of ID, but since she played ball and actually exhibited genuine manners, I waited for her while she looked through her purse until she found it.

When it was time for her picture, I pressed the button, took the photo, rotated the screen, and showed her the shot. It was a routine gesture that I must have made a million times, but I wasn't expecting what came next.

The woman looked at the screen and began to cry. "I'm sorry. I just." She paused. "The chemo's really fucked up my hair. It's hard for me sometimes to see it."

My mom had been going through this, too. For her the worst thing was not being able to eat. At one point I had spent hours at the stove making my mother risotto, her favorite. But when she ate it, she began to cry. She couldn't stand the mush in her mouth. The flavor. My mother pushed the plate away, then said, "All I taste is blood."

"This camera isn't forgiving," I told the woman in front of me now. "It's not you. It's just the computer."

She'd started to cry harder, so I found some Kleenex in my purse and passed it to her through the window.

"You know what? Forget it. Forget this picture. Let's get rid of it." I turned the screen back toward me. "Let's try again."

She'd closed her eyes and put one hand over her chest, the other over her mouth, and in this way it looked as if she were praying.

"You ready? How about now?"

She opened her eyes and nodded.

"I want you to look directly at the dot. Yup, just like that. Beautiful. Now lift your chin up a little bit and smile."

She followed the directions, and I snapped the shot.

Afterwards, I looked at the picture hopefully. But the smile looked forced, and she was gritting her teeth as if she couldn't breathe.

"It didn't work," I told her, deleting the picture. "Let's try again."

"Oh, don't worry about it," she said. "Don't trouble yourself." Then she smiled the way she did when she said good morning, and I clicked the mouse.

Quickly, the pixels shifted across that half a second. "There! We got it."

I turned the screen around so she could see the photo. This time the harsh glint of the fluorescent light didn't flash against her scalp. Instead, the camera captured the wide energy of her eyes. The generous smile. And I hoped that, looking at the picture, she could see it too. All the things that chemo could never take away from her.

* * *

One morning, I was running late to the ferry because Danny was not having it. The beginning of his teeth were cutting through his gums, so for the past week he'd been inconsolable. I needed to skip the shower and cajole him while my mother stood there, making all types of funny faces until he accepted her arms.

I made the boat by seconds. As the doors slid shut behind me, I followed the 7:00 a.m. crowd onto the mouth of the boat, where a thin fog hung around the ramp connecting the ferry to the pier. Inside, I had to hustle. The boat was so packed that people were sitting on the stairs. Normally, I would have just stood, but the morning drama with the baby and the run for the boat had left me exhausted.

When I did find an open space it was next to the loudmouth lawyer, same blue tie but free of yolk. And, of course, he was on the phone. Though I was too tired to care.

I waved a hand in front of him and pointed to the empty space beside him so that he could move a little bit, to which he sighed and shifted over begrudgingly.

"Thanks," I said. "Look, what a gentleman."

But he was so worked up on the phone that he didn't hear me. His cheeks were flushed. "You know what the sad part is, Sarita?" Then he lowered his voice. "I knew he was going to pull some shit like that. Ten years as a lawyer, and it never fails. People always do desperate things in desperate situations."

Which of course made me think about Michael, the desperation part, and how when I'd told him about Danny, he looked at me and said, "So what are you trying to do here, Julie?"

We were sitting there beside each other on the deck, looking out at the dark water blending into the sky. I stood there, quiet. I felt like he'd knocked me in the fucking chest.

"You must think I'm real stupid, huh?"

Then he cut me off completely.

Didn't pick up my phone calls or answer my emails, so that at one point

I got so frantic I drove all the way to Tottenville after work and showed up at his house, this ugly expensive new town home positioned right at the curve of a cul-de-sac, connected to three other houses with the same white aluminum siding and gray roof.

Once there I watched his wife laughing on the steps, gossiping with a neighbor before going inside. She had long, straight, almost black hair that reached her waist. And I was surprised. The woman was much prettier than me. The way Michael used to talk about her, you would never know it. I couldn't imagine why Michael would want to sleep with me instead of her.

I sat there for a couple of minutes with the air conditioner on full blast, my thighs sticking to the seat, until an old man knocked on my window asking me to move because I was blocking his driveway.

So I turned the car around and left.

* * *

At night, while Danny crawled around the coffee table and tried to stand up, my mother told me, "You underestimate yourself." She got like this sometimes after too many hours of Dr. Phil.

I picked up her unfinished plate of lasagna and laughed it off. "I don't underestimate myself, Ma."

"I just think you have so many skills. You were always so much smarter than Kathy's daughter. Jesus, you had to teach her how to use her LEGOs. Remember that? And now look who's the doctor."

My mother was always talking about people becoming doctors. That was the way she was.

I moved into the kitchen to start the dishes, turning the water on to block out her voice as she admonished Danny for reaching toward the little eyebrowless Precious Moments figurines she'd arranged on the end table: "No, don't do that, baby. Don't touch that. No good. Bad."

When I had gotten pregnant with Danny, I gave my mother the news at an Applebee's and started to blubber right there next to a table of teenagers singing out "Happy Birthday."

She looked at me and said, "It'll be okay, baby. We don't need anybody else." Then reached across the table and held my hand.

Of course, she didn't imagine then that she would get sick.

"Look at me, Julie," she said. "Have we ever needed anybody else?"

"No, never."

And to this day, even though she is gone, I don't think anybody in the world ever loved or understood me as much as my mother.

* * *

The next day, on the way back home to the Island from work while the boat was getting ready to dock, I heard the lawyer, my morning commute nemesis, before I saw him. Phone tucked between his shoulder and chin, a steaming black cup of coffee in hand with no lid. I stood at least four people behind him in order to avoid any interaction, but as luck would have it, the crowd moved in such a way that I found myself standing right beside him. A woman with her carriage stopped abruptly because her daughter had dropped a bottle, and when she bent down to pick it up the lawyer bumped into her and his hot coffee spilt sideways all over my coat.

"Oh my god, miss. I am so sorry," he kept saying, holding his hands out in apology.

And this is where I finally lost it. "Can't you look where the fuck you're going? Jesus, who walks around the boat with no lid on their coffee?"

The surrounding crowd was becoming irritated with the both of us as they made their way around our argument.

"Come on, lady, give me a break. I said I'm sorry." Then he offered me a greasy napkin streaked with ketchup from the bag holding his bacon, egg, and cheese.

Which was when it all happened.

A noise roared and ripped through the air as if a bomb had exploded.

The floor and the walls vibrated, and all of us jerked forward. From a distant spot in the front of the boat, people started to scream, and it took me a moment to realize that the boat was crashing into the pier. The concrete and wood of the dock were tearing into the vessel.

The lawyer's eyes widened as his phone fell from underneath his chin. "Move," he shouted.

My whole body was shaking, and at first, I couldn't go. My legs felt like they'd been deflated, but then the lawyer yanked my arm and pulled me away from the falling debris. Behind us the dock continued to eat the boat, cutting through the seats and the walls and the windows and the bodies of passengers who stood too close to the front and couldn't get away fast enough from the advancing metal.

At one point somebody knocked me down while they were running. And as I fell, my hand slid along the lawyer's wrist. He turned around and grabbed my elbow again to straighten me back up. And we took off.

But if he would have left me there like that, if I would have stayed down on the floor of the boat, if he would have kept on running, the pier would have cut me in half.

After the boat finally stopped, all of us crowded to the furthest edge of the vessel and waited. We thought we were sinking or that maybe the boat had been under some terrorist attack. The lawyer stood beside me searching for his cell phone, which he'd lost when we were running.

"Unfuckingbelievable," he said. "Oh, somebody is definitely getting sued."

* * *

Much later we learned that the pilot, whose back had been throbbing for days, took too many painkillers and, exhausted, had fallen asleep while navigating the boat. Since he was the only one in the pilot house, nobody had slowed the ferry down when it was time to dock. Instead, it went on at full speed and didn't stop.

Immediately after the crash, the pilot went home and tried to kill himself. Unsuccessfully, though. He survived and ended up doing three years in prison. But what stays with me always is not the pilot's story, or the way he cried during the trial, or the bloodied bodies, or even the victims' families. What I still think about sometimes, almost fifteen years later, is running away from the pier, and how when I fell it was Andrew who bent down to help me stand up. Sometimes in my dreams, I am still running away, except this time I am trying to escape this tall quick wave of darkness.

Every now and then, remembering it, I'll tell Andrew, "Oh man, I hated you. Sometimes I still can't believe that you stopped."

And always he'll kiss me on the side of the head and say something like, "Come on, what type of asshole do you think I am?" Then, while turning off a light before bed, or placing a hand on my knee in the car, or while running hot water over a stack of dirty dishes after dinner, he'll say, "Accept it, Jul. Sometimes, people are not as ugly as you think."

Acknowledgments

I am grateful to the editors of the journals where some of these stories, in slightly altered forms, first appeared:

Afro Hispanic Review, “Do Now”

BOAAT, “You Are a Strange Imitation of a Woman,” published as Gloria Clemente

District Lit, “Great Kills”

New Madrid, “Underneath the Water You Could Actually Hear Bells,” published as Gloria Clemente

Pank, “As Luck Would Have It”

Thank you to my mother the master teacher and my father the storyteller. To all of my sisters, whom I love so very much and who put me in check and continuously remind me not to play myself both in real life and on the page. Thank you especially to BB, who would read my stories late at night while she was trying to put her five-month and three-year-old children to bed and who corrected my many versions of “As Luck Would Have It.” BB, you could have been listening to “Baby Shark” for the fifteenth time, but you chose to help your old sister out and teach her how to use Twitter. That was very nice of you.

Thank you to Susan Kenney, with whom I took my first fiction workshop almost fifteen years ago and who has continued to teach and encourage me ever since.

Thank you to Emma Garcia, whose Latino literature course changed my life as a writer and who was the first person to introduce me to Gloria Anzaldúa.

Thank you to my mentors and teachers at Vanderbilt: Lorraine López, who has believed in my work and advocated for me since I landed in Nashville; Tony Earley, who made me love metaphor; and Nancy Reisman, whose workshop taught me to examine all of the different possibilities in my stories. Thank you to Kate Daniels for all that she taught me about poetry and Peter Guralnick for teaching me that there are no rules.

Thank you to all of my brilliant professors at the University of Nebraska–Lincoln. To Kwame Dawes, who reminded me that music is just as important in a story as it is in a poem. Thank you to Jonis Agee, who gave me probably the truest advice about writing: "Just keep pushing out the pages." To Timothy Schaffert, who, when I was feeling down about writing and useless in general, got me back on track, and to Luis Othoniel Rosa Rodriguez, whose resistance to bullshit inspires me to be honest. To Chigozie Obioma for helping our workshop think about syntax. To Celeste González de Bustamante for her class on moral geographies and borders, which greatly influenced this book. These stories also would not have been possible if I had not taken Writing Bootcamp during the summer of 2018 with Stacey Waite, who reminded me to get the fuck off Facebook and finish my collection. To Dr. Jeannette Jones, who, when she found me overwhelmed with coursework and teaching, told me, "Claire, prioritize that manuscript." Finally, thank you to Joy Castro for her wisdom and mentorship.

I also want to thank my friends and fellow writers, who got me through this collection, especially Destiny Birdsong, who read these stories over and over again and who has always had my back and made me laugh. You are a sister to me. Thank you to Damion Meyer, who especially helped me toward the end of this manuscript as I nervously kept on rearranging the stories and who put up with all of my neuroses. I would have not gotten this collection done without you. Now, go finish your book!

Thank you to my good friend Lee Conell for her countless emails commiserating over writing, teaching, and our perpetual quest for free food. Thanks to the savvy Janet Thielke, who always shows up on time with professional advice and good literary gossip. Thank you to Angel Garcia, whose friendship has helped me get through the hard moments of writing and just being a PhD student in general. To Tenaja Jordan, who rescued my drafts many times with a fresh pair of eyes in the middle of the night. To David Henson, who encouraged me to keep on writing these stories and whose faith and excellent eye helped me revise them. Thank you to Jill Schepmann: her kindness makes me want to be a better person not only on the page, but also in the world. And thank you to all my fellow writers at UNL and Vanderbilt, especially Simon Han, Anna Silverstein, Reid Douglass, Maggie Zebracka, Cara Dees, Chris Adamson, Jenna Williams, Ricardo Zamorano Baez, Edgar Kunz, Sara Strong, Marysa LaRowe, Rebecca Bernard, Alexander Ramirez, Ilana Masad, Katherine Schwartman, Katherine Pierson, Linda Garcia Merchant, Belinda G. Acosta, Katie Francisco, Audrey Schutte, Jeremy Caldwell, and Adrienne Christian. Thank you to the people I worked with at the Gerard Carter Center in Staten Island, especially my Young Men's Initiative kids, who inspired me and kept me laughing while I wrote many of these stories.

Many thanks to my agent, Jane von Mehren, for her expertise and insight. And to the good folks at Johns Hopkins University Press, especially Wyatt Prunty and Hilary Jacqmin, for their wonderful feedback and careful editing.

At some point during the process of writing this collection, I've had friends who helped me outside the page. They nurtured me and got me to a place where I could write again. Thank you to Katherine Delfina Perez, Nichelle and Germanie Ogiste, Stephen Garguilo, Douglas Macon, Cindy Choung, Francine Rivera, Caitlin McGuire, Ozzy Ramirez, Kadeen Raphael, Zen Glasser, Jen Wilkins, the Feliz sisters, and the Maradiaga and Ouaaz families. I love you.

Fiction Titles in the Series

Guy Davenport, *Da Vinci's Bicycle*
Stephen Dixon, *14 Stories*
Jack Matthews, *Dubious Persuasions*
Guy Davenport, *Tatlin!*
Joe Ashby Porter, *The Kentucky Stories*
Stephen Dixon, *Time to Go*
Jack Matthews, *Crazy Women*
Jean McGarry, *Airs of Providence*
Jack Matthews, *Ghostly Populations*
Jack Matthews, *Booking in the Heartland*
Jean McGarry, *The Very Rich Hours*
Steve Barthelme, *And He Tells the Little Horse the Whole Story*
Michael Martone, *Safety Patrol*
Jerry Klinkowitz, *Short Season and Other Stories*
James Boylan, *Remind Me to Murder You Later*
Frances Sherwood, *Everything You've Heard Is True*
Stephen Dixon, *All Gone: 18 Short Stories*
Jack Matthews, *Dirty Tricks*
Joe Ashby Porter, *Lithuania*
Robert Nichols, *In the Air*
Ellen Akins, *World Like a Knife*
Greg Johnson, *A Friendly Deceit*
Guy Davenport, *The Jules Verne Steam Balloon*
Guy Davenport, *Eclogues*
Jack Matthews, *Storyhood as We Know It and Other Tales*
Stephen Dixon, *Long Made Short*
Jean McGarry, *Home at Last*
Jerry Klinkowitz, *Basepaths*
Greg Johnson, *I Am Dangerous*
Josephine Jacobsen, *What Goes without Saying: Collected Stories*
Jean McGarry, *Gallagher's Travels*
Richard Burgin, *Fear of Blue Skies*
Avery Chenoweth, *Wingtips*
Judith Grossman, *How Aliens Think*
Glenn Blake, *Drowned Moon*
Robley Wilson, *The Book of Lost Fathers*
Richard Burgin, *The Spirit Returns*
Jean McGarry, *Dream Date*
Tristan Davies, *Cake*
Greg Johnson, *Last Encounter with the Enemy*
John T. Irwin and Jean McGarry, eds., *So the Story Goes: Twenty-Five Years of the Johns Hopkins Short Fiction Series*
Richard Burgin, *The Conference on Beautiful Moments*
Max Apple, *The Jew of Home Depot and Other Stories*
Glenn Blake, *Return Fire*
Jean McGarry, *Ocean State*
Richard Burgin, *Shadow Traffic*
Robley Wilson, *Who Will Hear Your Secrets?*
William J. Cobb, *The Lousy Adult*
Tracy Daugherty, *The Empire of the Dead*
Richard Burgin, *Don't Think*
Glenn Blake, *The Old and the Lost*
Lee Conell, *Subcortical*
Adrianne Harun, *Catch, Release*
Claire Jimenez, *Staten Island Stories*